fairy dust FUMBLE

PETE FANNING

Immortal Works LLC
1505 Glenrose Drive
Salt Lake City, Utah 84104
Tel: (385) 202-0116

© 2021 Pete Fanning
www.petefanning.com

Cover Art by Lenore Stutznegger
www.lenorestutz.com

All rights reserved, including the right to reproduce this book or portions thereof in any form whatsoever. For more information email contact@immortal-works.com or visit http://www.immortal-works.com/contact/.

This book is a work of fiction. Names, characters, businesses, organizations, places, events and incidents either are the product of the author's imagination or are used fictitiously. Any resemblance to actual persons, living or dead, events, or locales is entirely coincidental.

ISBN 978-1-953491-25-1 (Paperback)
ASIN B096Q6V3F3 (Kindle)

For Anne, who puts up with my many misadventures, every single day.

Chapter 1
Cursed

It's game day. I throw on my powder blue Panthers jersey and tuck it into my jeans. Only it's too bulky and it bunches up at the waist, and so I untuck it but then it looks like a dress. I settle on something in between, the half-tuck, then check myself out in the mirror. I work on my scowl until I accidentally bite the inside of my cheek.

I tell myself again that things are fine, just fine. And for three or four steps down the hallway things *are* fine, right up until I find my mom and my little sister in the kitchen, huddled at the table, shaking their heads and stifling laughs.

My little sister reaches out to the phone—my phone!—and touches the screen. "See, right there. He tips forward and from there it's all over."

"Poor thing," Mom offers. My sister shrugs, then touches the screen to resume the video. Sure enough, like an old cartoon, a clash of cymbals followed by the tinkly clatter of xylophone keys fills the kitchen. Only this is no cartoon they're watching.

I step out from the doorway. "Hey, what are you guys doing with my phone?"

They whirl around, eyes wide with caffeine and guilt. And just like that, any hopes last night was some strange dream that left my back sore is squashed to bug guts.

Abby tilts her head and lets out a sigh. "If only you would have listened to me, Colton."

I ignore her and look at Mom, pointing to the phone. "What are you guys watching?"

Mom steps forward, using her soft voice, the breaking-bad-news voice. "Honey, I think you should..."

I snatch my phone from Abby. Again, I don't have time for Mom's pity or my sister's advice—advice I'm getting in heaps as I see the video titled, *Epic Fairy Fail*. And there's me on stage, frozen in failure, wearing tights and holding a wand, no less.

The tights, the wand, it's part of this New Faces theater thing at school—a trick to round up suckers and put them onstage to make fools of themselves. Mission accomplished. This year's title is *Gypsies and Fairies*, only there's just one fairy. Me.

Abby sits up straight and sets her arms out. "What were you doing, anyway? Walking like that on the stage. I mean, what is that?"

"I was flitting. Fairies flit."

Her hand doesn't make it to her mouth in time to stop the giggles.

"Abby," Mom coos. Her way of scolding my sister. Abby shrugs.

"Well, I could've helped, you know."

She gets back to arranging her playing cards spread out in front of her. Cards she thinks could have "protected me" from falling off the stage last night at rehearsals.

Abby is convinced I'm *cursed*. I remind her I'm on the football team. She reminds me I'm third string and never really play. "Still, I'm on the team."

"Yeah. Nice jersey."

It never ends around here. I go for the Captain Crunch and pour half of it on the counter because it's hard to roll your eyes and pour cereal at the same time. I sweep the scatter of cereal into my bowl, dump in the milk, snatch my phone, and lumber towards the table. Abby won't hear it. She stacks the twos and threes and so on in neat piles.

"When are you going to admit it?"

"When you admit you're not a witch."

She holds up a Jack of hearts. "For protection. Put it in your back pocket."

The last thing I need is help from my precocious little sister. It's bad enough she's skipped fifth grade and is only a single grade behind me now, it's even worse that because she gets straight A's, her antics are tolerated. Because I get straight C's, my life is under a microscope. Especially after play rehearsal last night.

I wipe back my hair and find a Captain Crunch stuck to my hand. "Please don't start with the Jacks. It's entirely too early for this."

"Suit yourself," she says with a giggle.

I shovel in three bites. Abby's smile reaches for her ears. I drop my spoon into the bowl. *Clank.* "What?"

She holds up the cards. "Get it? *Suit* yourself?"

Mom rubs her eyes and turns for the coffee maker. I get back to my phone. "I need to make sure that video didn't—" My phone buzzes. A text from Zach.

Dude ur famous.

Another buzz. This time a YouTube link. The same one my mother and sister were watching. This is not good.

Mom glances over her shoulder. "So how is your backside, sweetie?"

Abby snorts. I'm tempted to scatter her neat little piles of cards. She likes to arrange the spell casters and the spell protectors or—jeez, I'm embarrassed I even know what she's doing. I shake my head, refusing to play this game. "I'm fine, thanks for your concern."

Wiping the milk from my chin, I take a breath, then click on the link. My screen is cracked and splotchy—long story—but after a quick insurance ad, I'm staring at the plush red curtains of the Peakland High auditorium where we rehearse.

Action! And there's me, blissful, ignorant, digital me, about to take a fall at play rehearsal last night. Watching it now it's even worse than I thought. A bumbling fairy, helpless to the fate that lay before him. Attracted to a fall like iron to a magnet.

Mom eases up behind me, her feet crunching on the trail of cereal I've left behind. "How many views does it have now?" she asks.

I can practically hear Mom and Abby grinning. One head over each shoulder. Sometimes I think they speak to each other through some kind of female telepathy. I turn around, and their eyes widen in unison.

"Twenty-two-hundred hits," Abby announces. Mom shushes her just in time for my grand performance. There I go with my wand, teetering and wobbling before the slip, flip, and tumble into a podium, plummeting off the stage, sending a ladder crashing into the xylophone.

Lots of giggling. In the video and at the table.

"Such a shame," Abby says in her Mom voice. "Theater is no place for a clumsy fairy."

This time Mom doesn't even try to hide her laugh. But she cuts it short and points to the screen. "Is that Lani Andrews?"

Abby scoffs. "Why else would he be in the play, as a fairy no less?"

This is too much. I pocket my phone, check the clock on the microwave. "Well, gotta go."

"Such a sweet girl. I always liked her," Mom says.

"Yeah. Colton *likes* her, too."

I get to my feet and glare at my sister. Mom gives my shoulder a squeeze. "Oh sweetie, don't worry, it was just an accident. It happens to your father all the time."

"Oh my gosh," Abby gushes. "Remember when Dad fell off the ladder hanging the Christmas lights?"

"Or when he got tangled up in the mini-blinds," Mom adds, and they're off, reliving every mishap, pointing and giggling. I ignore them and get back to my phone, 2,268 now. I scroll to the comment section. (Tip: if you ever find yourself on YouTube, do not read the comments. Some things are better not seen.) Mom and Abby continue to live it up.

"What about when he hit himself in the head with the golf club?" Mom says, abandoning any hint of neutrality. From there they go on about the day Dad came home with that big hulking lump on his head. He'd been golfing with some guys at work, and well, the details are sketchy.

"The Clutts family curse," Abby says like a wise old crone. "I'm sure glad I'm protected. Aren't you, Mom?"

Mom sips her coffee and nods, lending legitimacy to Abby's foolishness. But I can't help myself. "So what about Dad?" I ask my sister, crossing my arms to hide the spread of chill bumps. "Why can't you 'protect' him?"

Abby holds up four jacks, tilting her head at me like I'm dense. "I'm afraid it's too late for Dad. He's too old and his curse is too strong." She leans in closer, getting all super dramatic. "But there's still hope for you. Maybe."

I scoff, but it's like I can't find my breath. Did I mention I hate curse talk? All the slips and scrapes over the years. Too many to count. Dad busting through the ceiling from the attic. His blackened fingernails whenever he uses a hammer, how he sometimes falls *up* the stairs. He spills and splatters, nicks and dents. Dad can crack fine china from three rooms away. And I'm his only son. Where Abby got the brains in the family, I inherited my father's dicey relationship with gravity.

"Colton," Mom says, breaking my trance, "just remember, the best thing we can do is to take caution. Slow down. That's what I tell your father. It's what Grandma told Papa. And what Great Grandma—"

"Mom, I got it."

"He's got it all right," Abby says, staring at my phone. She swipes and replays the video, and yep, this time I distinctly hear bells. And howls of laughter. Abby clicks her teeth. "He's got it bad."

I pat down my pockets. "How did you—" I snatch my phone from her again.

Being reminded that you've been hit with a family curse is not the best way to start your day, but neither is finding your stage tumble on YouTube. Anyway, I refuse to let some stupid superstition keep me down. I start for the sink but trip over the chair and the milk in my cereal bowl drenches my face. Abby and Mom gawk at me.

"Oh come on, that could happen to anyone," I say, blowing milk bubbles with "happen." I wipe my face with my shirt.

"Uh huh." Abby fans the deck of cards.

I stomp off for the bathroom, away from the snorting and giggling in the kitchen. A couple thousand views, that's not a whole lot, maybe no one at school saw it. Who am I kidding? I'm so dead.

I wash my face, work on my scowl again. Another half tuck of my jersey and I'm good to go. I toss a quick wave to Mom as I charge out the door.

Outside, a beautiful day is taking shape. I fiddle with the straps of my book bag and take in the fresh air. Sometimes I wait for Abby, but after all the laughing, the little thief can take her broom to school for all I care.

The leaves scrape along the street with my steps, a cool breeze finds my neck. I cut through a couple of yards, get grass on my shoes, and come out one street over, at Zach's house.

For the millionth time I tell myself it can't be that bad. And that's when I check my back pocket, where, just like yesterday, I find the four jacks. Maybe I should be more thankful Abby goes to all the trouble. Instead, just like yesterday, I toss them in Zach's trash can.

The door opens and Zach steps outside. He's about to start in on the video when he stops, looks at me, then to the trash can, and shakes his shaggy blond hair from his eyes.

"How does she do that, anyway?"

"I have no idea."

Chapter 2
Mr. Popular

My football jersey hasn't yet elevated me to baller status the way I'd hoped. But today, getting to school, I gaze across the vast sea of shiny cars that separates Peakland High School from Peakland Middle School, it's clear things are going to be different.

I'm suddenly a very popular dude. From the moment I walk into school, everyone is smirking and patting me on the back. I'm the center of attention. Eighth graders ask me if I had a nice trip, some seventh graders want my autograph. Even the lowly sixth graders point and whisper. At lunch I'm given a standing ovation.

Zach, however, is giddy with my newfound fame. We meet back up at my locker before sixth period. His eyes are wide and he's smiling like crazy. He shakes his phone in my face. "It's everywhere. Mr. Mengie even let us watch it on the Smartboard."

I shoot him a look. "In history class?"

He nods, fiddling with the tassels of the scarf he's wearing over his RUN DMC t-shirt. My best friend is constantly switching up his style, sometimes by lunch he's gone through as many as three wardrobe changes. "Yep, and that fall was *historic.*"

"Hey, Clutts." More passing smirks. It doesn't help that our prestigious play director thought it would be a good idea for the cast to get "better acclimated" with the characters they were playing. For me this means walking around Peakland Middle School with purple fairy wings, wand, and a vial of fairy dust in my pocket. So far, I've only gotten acclimated with humiliation.

The only good news is that play practice has been cancelled —something about a staff meeting. Not that it makes my life any easier. Fine with me, after a day of unoriginal heckling (walk much?), I'm ready to hurry home where I can veg out and gorge on snacks before the football game. If I've learned anything this season, it's that riding the bench on an empty stomach is no fun.

With Mom and Dad at work, I've got the house all to myself. Abby's at one of her too-many-to-count extracurriculars. Because of her smarts, my parents roll with Abby's witchiness. My dad calls it Goth. Again, I'm not sure if it does her any favors in middle school, but when it comes to the curse—if there is such a thing, which there's totally not—she's been spared. Anything she does, she does well—violin, dance, chess, science —so my parents ignore the fact that she would have been burned at the stake a few centuries ago.

After snarfing half a box of Cheez-Its while pacing through the house, I get dressed, hop on my bike, and head back to school.

Coach Jackson is already out on the field, lugging equipment out from the locker room. He sees me coming and grins. "Hey Colt, how's my quarterback?"

What he really means is, "How's my third string quarterback who I will never, ever let pass the ball?"

Coach played college ball back in the day and takes football seriously. He's gray around the temples, but don't let it fool you, the guy's still ripped. It's not hard to tell where his son—our starting quarterback, Trayvon—gets his build.

"I'm good, Coach."

"Great day for football," he says, taking in our little field like it's the dawn of the Super Bowl. The truth is that a middle school football game gets about as much attention as a chess match. Maybe less.

"Cold Cuts!"

I turn to find our starting quarterback strutting to the field. Trayvon Jackson is taller, faster, and bigger than me or any else on our team. More importantly, Trayvon has the distinct advantage of being able to run and jump over defenders without falling on his facemask—which I hear is crucial when it comes to football.

"Hey Trayvon, how many touchdowns you think you'll score today?" I ask, continuing my strategy of complimenting him into liking me. Mixed results so far, but he gives me a bright smile, the one reserved for post-game interviews.

"At least two. Why, are you trying to get into the game today?"

I shrug. Like I said, I'm third string. That means I don't play until the fourth quarter, and then only if we're absolutely crushing the opposing team. But looking around, there's no sign of Ben, the second-string quarterback, which makes my breath a little jittery.

More of the guys arrive and Coach Jackson claps his hands like a starter pistol cracking through the sky. "All right fellas, let's go warm up."

Clear skies and a tiny breeze. The late afternoon is cool in the shade and warm in the sun. A perfect fall day to ride the pine and watch a football game. Our opponent, Hamersley Middle, storms the field and begins warm-ups. I look back and find a few new heads in the bleacher section. The scouting report on Hamersley is that they're big but slow. They've won a game and lost a game. We're one and one as well, our loss coming when Trayvon was out with the flu. Coincidentally, I didn't play that game either, so there's that.

We spread out and begin our stretching. Parents file in,

groups of families dotting the bleachers, little kids playing tag along the track. I shield the evening sun, looking for Dad, but when I bend down to touch my toes I notice a good-sized hole in the knee of my pants. Great. Max, our playful husky mix has a habit of nibbling on sweaty football clothes. Dirty socks, underwear—I've even caught him chewing on my mouthpiece like a piece of bubble gum.

"Oh man, Cold Cuts! My favorite fairy boy!"

Phillip Jenkins. Great again. I sigh, thinking how I might as well get it over with. Phillip is most likely the source of the now world-famous YouTube video. Oh, and the name Cold Cuts? He came up with that little gem all by himself.

"Yeah, you know, just keeping things interesting," I say, continuing my other strategy of laughing things off. It must be working, because the whole team is cracking up.

"Well, great job. I mean, dude, I stop by the auditorium to talk to my girl, and there you are falling off stage. I'm just glad I got it on video," he says, digging his phone out of a place normally reserved for a cup. Gross.

Warm-ups are forgotten as the team huddles closer to watch the video I now recognize by sound alone. And this is when our assistant coach, Coach Barber, barges out to the field. "Hey, ya'll watching that video of Colt falling off stage and crashing into the speakers? Come on, bring it in. I've got to see that again," he says with a chuckle.

Coach Barber is in every way the opposite of Coach Jackson. He's big and round with a big old belly and floppy cheeks. And where Coach Jackson is defensive minded, Coach Barber is all about getting the ball down the field. They often clash on strategy.

By kickoff, the bleachers are nearly a third full, easily our biggest crowd of the year. I settle in at my spot at the end of the bench with the other scrubs, content to stay out of the way. I turn and look for Mom or Dad but still don't see them. Maybe they got stuck in traffic. Not sure why they bother anyway.

Out on the field, Trayvon wastes no time finding the end zone, zigging left, then right, before tearing down the sidelines for an opening score. The closest person to him is our own running back, Luke Patterson. Trayvon trots back to the sidelines, ripping off his helmet with a big grin on his face. "That's one, Colt."

At halftime, we're up by twenty. We don't even bother to take it in to the locker room, instead just hanging around laughing and talking. Trayvon is without a helmet and looks to be done for the afternoon. Not good for me. The thought of getting in the game has my knees knocking and my feet like icebergs.

Zach plops down on the bench beside me. "Dude, whaddya think?" he says, nodding back to the bleachers. Security is kind of slack at our football games, so Zach comes and goes as he pleases. I glance back, past McKenzie Cooper and the rest of the cheerleaders. Impressive, I'll admit. I've never seen so many people down at the field. It makes my palms slick. Another look at the scoreboard, then down the bench. No sign of Ben.

Gulp.

"I think the crowd is here to see the newest viral sensation," Zach says with a nudge. "You're up past five thousand hits now."

Just like that he whips out his phone, as though I need to see *that* right now. I jump as Coach Jackson barks my name. "Colt, get ready. You're going in for the third quarter."

Zap goes my heart. "Um, what?"

"Yes!" Zach jumps up, nearly fumbling his phone. "This is it, your big chance!"

Coach waves him off. "Back to the bleachers, Zach."

"Got it, Coach," he says. "Good luck, Colt!"

Then he's off, walking backwards, his phone aimed at yours truly. He gives me a thumbs up as he ducks back to the safety of the bleachers. Coach kneels beside me. "Okay son, I'd like to rest Trayvon, show some sportsmanship. So get out there."

Not exactly the pep-talk of the year, explaining how I'm going in as a favor to the other team, but that's Coach Jackson for you. The guy tells it like it is. I nod, look down at the helmet between my feet, stuffed with a Doctor Pepper and a half a bag of Fritos. Riding the bench, I've found that a football helmet makes a decent cooler.

Coach Jackson storms off to chew out the defense. They've given up a couple first downs and he wants to get them back on track.

I jump as Coach Barber lays a bear paw on my shoulder pad. "Okay kid, uh, you're up."

I open my mouth to tell him I can't. Really, find someone else. But Coach Barber shrugs, like, *Don't look at me, kid. This is Coach Jackson's idea.*

The crowd gets going as the ref whistles for the second half to get underway. Okay then. I get my rubbery legs working.

Here goes nothing.

My hands tremble as I try to buckle my chin strap. At the sideline, Coach Jackson's finger finds my facemask and brings me into his gravitational pull. "You got this, Colt. Just hand the ball to Luke and stay out of the way. You'll be fine, all right?"

He releases me and I nod, peeking up to the stands where, wouldn't you know it, there's Mom and Dad, cheering me on. Dad's on his feet, pumping his giant #1 foam finger like a maniac, wobbling like one of those Mr. Wiggles inflatables outside the used car lot. Mom wisely yanks him down to safety before injury strikes. With a breath, I set foot onto the field, and inevitably, my doom.

First of all, my cleats are a yard sale find and a size too big.

My dad, whose love for a deal supersedes his son's safety, told me to, *roll with it*. He figured I'd grow into them soon enough. Until I do, he suggests wearing an extra pair of socks to cover the difference. Thing is, up until now, it's never mattered because I was never going to play. In fact, I'd worn my Sperries to the last game and wasn't exactly astonished when no one noticed. But now, charging onto the field to lead my team to victory, something catches the hollow toe of my shoe.

Splat.

I fall like a sack of bolts. In plain view on the field. Coach Jackson's on me in an instant, jerking me up by my collar. I stumble around some, like a fighter who's just been walloped.

"Might want to tie those laces, kid."

Tie my laces? I can't get my helmet twisted back around to see anything. I think I have a Frito in my ear. Coach straightens me out, and eventually we get both shoes laced up and he points me in the right direction and sends me out to the slaughter. My only hope is that with it being the second half, with the offenses and the defenses taking their places on the field, maybe no one—

"OMG, dude. I knew you'd come through. I'm so posting that."

Phillip waits for me at the huddle, recording it all with his jock cam. The crowd chuckles continuously, like one big studio audience on a sitcom. They've got jokes too, applauding and whistling as I brush myself off. Even our own players on the bench break into a standing ovation. Coach tells them to cool it. And so with nothing left to do, I yank on my socks and hit the huddle.

"All right, Jumbo Right, twenty-six Power on three."

"Dude, you have grass in your facemask."

"Yeah, you already got sacked and the play hasn't started."

Dad likes to buy me these used sports books, autobiographies and motivational stuff. So I know how any good quarterback takes his team by the reins. But what if his team is watching a video of said quarterback falling down right there in the huddle? Hmm, going to have to improvise.

"Guys, come on, I just—"

The ref blows the whistle. Delay of game. Coach Jackson nods me along, clapping vigorously and shouting what he considers encouragement. Trayvon stands beside his dad, arms crossed, his clean jersey shimmering under the lights. Meanwhile I'm already filthy and I haven't run a play. We back up five yards and try again. Things are off to a wonderful start.

I call the play. Jumbo Right. Again. By now the crowd is getting noisy. Lots of laughing, it's a regular circus atmosphere in the stands. Even the Hamersley guys are snickering. Pretty cocky for a bunch of guys down by three touchdowns. I start the count, "Ready, set..." I swing my head left then right. The wind picks up. A light gust blows in from behind. Like, really blowing in from behind.

Someone taps my shoulder. Luke, our running back, cackling so hard I can barely make out what he's trying to tell me, says, "Dude...your...pants."

I run a hand around my backside where I should feel polyester, but instead find a gaping hole about the size of a football. That explains the draft.

Another whistle. Delay of game.

Again.

I motion to Coach Jackson, who I think is actually grinning. Trayvon is draped all over Coach Barber, yukking it up with everyone else. And by everyone I mean both sides of stands, pointing and laughing and otherwise having the time of their lives. Even Mom has a hand clasped to her mouth, but I'm pretty sure there's a smile under there too.

I try to turn around, check it out myself, but with my helmet on I only stagger and twist and it sends everyone into hysterics.

Only one thing to do. I drop to the ground and scoot towards the sidelines. The crowd goes nuts.

I'm going to kill Max. It isn't just the knee pads he's been chewing. When Coach helped me up earlier they must have split all the way through. And now I'm left with no choice but to crab-walk back to the bench. The ref tosses another flag.

Coach ushers me in and helps me to my feet. "Shake it off Clutts. We'll see if we can find a spare pair of pants around here."

I drag my drafty butt back to the bench. Luke takes over at quarterback and on the very next play the crowd is cheering once again. I glance up as he trots in for a score.

Great.

Chapter 3
Pie in the Sky

On the way home, Dad breaks the silence in the goofy, aww-shucks way of his. "Come on, Colton, you just need pizza, that's all."

What I need is a face transplant. I can't show the one I've got at school, not after following up the stage-dive with a fall-on-my-face-wardrobe-malfunction-crab walk at our football game (which we won 34-8, by the way).

It's just Dad and me and my bike stuffed in the back. Mom drove separately because she had to show a house over in Oak Point (*Show the house what?* Dad always says). I look him over, wondering how in the world we're related. We don't have much in common, not counting the clumsy. He's the only dad I know who doesn't watch the NFL, or sports at all, if you don't count spelling bees. In fact, he has no interest in football other than cheering me on while I ride the bench. Anything with a ball, my dad avoids. And after tonight, I totally get it.

We pull into the shopping center near Michelangelo's Pizza, where the team usually meets up on game nights. "Can we just get it to go?" I ask, pretty sure that my three delay-of-game penalties will be the main topic of discussion.

Dad glances over at me and nods. "Sure thing, sport."

"Dad."

"What? Oh yeah, sorry. Sure thing, *Colton*."

Man. What a nerd. He hands me the phone and I call in two large pineapple and pepperoni pizzas. Michelangelo's is the best. The wood-fired crust is perfect. It's so good that even with a bruised and shattered ego, I'm willing to risk being seen in the parking lot.

Dad pulls out some cash, but then yanks it back. "If you see Coach Jackson let him know that you're not staying."

"Wait. Can't you go get it?" The whole point of getting the pizza to go was so that I would *not* see anyone. Like I said about Dad, he's never played sports. He was in the marching band (I've seen the pictures and it's *exactly* what you'd expect). He doesn't understand locker room dynamics.

"No way. Better to go face it now, bud."

My dad is all about doing the right thing, being a stand-up guy, facing adversity and blah blah. But he's sort of got a point about facing it now, getting it over with, and so I take the bills and scan the entrance, planning to rush in like a ninja—get in, get out—and escape with the goods. I've covered my holey pants with an old pair of sweatpants Dad just happens to keep stashed in the van.

So far, so good. I make my move, creeping from van to sidewalk, from sidewalk to store. Success.

Inside, the deliciously warm aroma of bread and cheese pokes awake my stomach. The smiley girl at the register asks for the name.

"Clutts."

"Butts?"

I sigh. "No, Clutts."

"Oh, right," she chuckles. She grabs two grease-spotted boxes and slides them on the counter. I hand her the cash. A quick glance around. Only a few diners. An older couple, some guy wearing a cowboy hat, a family with three noisy kids at the window. No sign of teammates. I pick up the pies, nod to the girl, and make a hasty escape.

With my hands under the warm box, my knees wobble

some as I breathe in the mouthwatering pizza smell. Easy does it. Carefully, I shift, trying to figure out the door when a guy approaches from outside and holds it open. I nod my thanks. Placing one careful foot in front of the next outside, I'm unable to see my feet but I know there's a curb there, somewhere. *There.* I'm thinking, hopping off to the street, *Disaster averted.*

In the van, Dad's on the phone, his hands flopping around like he's fighting a nest of bees. Probably work. When he sees me coming, he leans over to open the door, and I'm *this* close when a car materializes out of thin air, flying in and pulling close to the curb with super-charged high beams. The lights do a number on my eyes, and it's with searing retinas I totally don't see the other van coming from the other direction.

Brakes screech. I nearly leap out of my clothes. I lose my footing on the speed bump and toss the two boxes above my head like I'm a contestant in a pizza juggling competition. Only I forget the juggling part. And the gravity part. Flat on my back, I hadn't heard anything about pizza in the forecast, but I look up to find it's raining pepperoni and pineapple pizza.

They paste me in hot gooey shame. A car door thumps. I detect voices, but there's cheese in my ears so it's hard to make out what's being said.

"Colton?"

I wipe my face. Stringy cheese like puppet strings stretches from my hands. My hair is warm and wet with clumps of pineapple. Red sauce promises to stain my jersey. And through the smear of it all is Lani Andrews, the lead gypsy in our play. A girl I first met in the fourth grade but who has recently morphed into a celestial being.

Behind her glasses, her big, brown eyes go wide with shock.

"Uh, hey," I mumble, playing it casual, or, as casual as wearing a pizza in the middle of the road will allow. Speaking of pizza, I'm surprised to see one of them is sort of still intact. The cheese is shifted over but it's not a total loss. Max will love it.

Lani falls to a knee, wipes a strand of hair from her face. "Um, are you okay?"

Can't imagine what I look like. But I can taste pizza sauce on my lips so things can't be awesome. At least Lani isn't laughing—so far as I can tell—unlike the heads hanging out of the car windows as traffic lines up in both directions. Great.

"Oh, um, yeah, I'm fine." I flick a pepperoni from my arm. Like that helps. A few Panthers jerseys approach from the sidewalk. Some girls, too. McKenzie Cooper and two other giggling cheerleaders bounce over to the scene.

I start to snatch up the partial pizza, thinking I can still cut my losses, get out of here without a show, until my dad comes clambering out of the van. A bad scene gets worse as he rushes over, and in true Clutts fashion, gets his feet tangled, and the next thing I know he's going down, slipping on the pizza on the pavement.

"Oh jeez, sorry," Dad says scrambling to his feet. His feet slide on the sauce and now there's quite a crowd checking us out. Dad's unfazed, even with pizza sauce down the leg of his Dockers. We Clutts guys are so used to falling that we hardly notice it at all anymore. "Colton, what happened, kiddo?"

Any hopes of going unnoticed go the way of the road-kill pizza. The team arrives in pairs, joining the crowd that now includes Lani, my dad, giggling cheerleaders, and a string of random people who've happened to pass. It doesn't help how the Quicker Renter mascot has moved in, thrusting his giant neon yellow arrow down on me, announcing my fall to the world like it's some one-time sale extravaganza.

Faces peer out of the window. Those brats in Michelangelo's have their noses to the glass, banging and pointing and laughing it up. And if that's not embarrassing enough, for me to be standing like a freak show out there head to toe in pizza goo, Dad has come rushing over, calling me *kiddo*.

"Nothing Dad, come on, let's go." I try to kick the pizza back into the box, so embarrassed I'm shaking. Not only that, I'm sweating and hot, or that could just be the pizza sauce on my forehead. Then comes Mr. Jock-Cam himself.

"Dude, you're like a YouTube machine. I'm going to have to hire a camera crew!"

Traffic crawls around the scene while a semi-circle of normal, clean, laughing kids gather around to gawk at Pizza Boy...Fairy Boy...Football Pants Boy. All of the above.

Eventually, people get over it and go about their business. Lani reaches over and plucks a pineapple off my shirt. "You like pineapple on your pizza, too? My favorite."

"Yeah," I manage, because I'm hardly feeling human at the moment. I run a hand through my hair, coming out with a fist full of tomato sauce.

Lani smiles. "Okay, well, don't forget rehearsal tomorrow. Mom and I are running into the craft store now." She tosses back her sandy blonde hair. She fixes her glasses, her eyes narrowing as she looks toward the curb where all the football players and cheerleaders are standing around, shaking their heads and laughing it up. "Huh, I completely forgot about the football game."

I breathe a sigh of relief. At least she didn't see what happened on the field. "Yeah, rehearsals. Nope, I won't forget," I say, still playing it cool. I kick some cheese off my shoe. Over on the sidewalk, McKenzie whispers something and the cheerleaders break into synchronized laughter before they spin off, blue and silver ribbons bouncing with their steps.

Traffic gets moving. Dad picks up a pizza box, says something about a refill. I stand off to the side, sticky and warm, watching Lani until she looks back at me with a smile and waves once again. Dad is just about to say something mortifying when I turn and drag myself to the van.

I'm still a mess, my jogging pants a tomato massacre, stained to the knee on one leg and all the way up the other. Climbing into the van I take a quick look around, hoping Dad thought to pack a back-up, back-up bag.

Chapter 4
Fairy Tales

At lunch the next day Zach informs me I'm up to ten thousand hits on my Epic Fairy Fail video plus another two thousand on the Football Fail video.

"'What a complete doofus'." Zach's smile widens as he rambles off the comments. I can't be sure, but he seems to be having a great time with my sudden popularity. And it's cool, we've been through a lot since the third grade when Zach moved to East Ridge. He even knows about the so-called curse. That said, he's laughing a little too hard at those comments.

"'Run much?'" He holds up a hand before I can protest. "Wait, here's a good one, sorta, 'Hey leave the guy alone, he obviously has some issues.'"

I drop my sandwich. "Look, will you do me a favor and read them quietly to yourself? I've had enough."

"Sure, no problem." Zach scrolls along, not so quietly cracking himself up. Finally, he pockets the phone and taps his hands on the lunch table. Unlike me, his voice is upbeat and without shame. "Hey, look at it this way, with Hillsdale up next, there's no way you're getting in the game."

"Thanks, I think?" I go for my sandwich again. Maybe it's all in my head, but I think my hands still smell like pizza sauce.

"Yeah, whatever I can do." Zach jabs at his entrée with his fork, a greenish chicken patty that looks like a stone. "Hey so, this Trayvon thing..."

Ugh. I'd rather him read the comments. Trayvon Jackson

isn't at school today. Zach says maybe he's out sick. But there are other rumors floating around. Rumors that, if true, could mean our football season is Kaput. I've already heard he's forgoing high school and going straight to college on scholarship. And while I'm not buying that, it's got me a little woozy, thinking I might be thrust into practice as a tackling dummy. But hey, at least people aren't talking about my videos.

After lunch I catch Lani in the hallway and she waves. A surge of hope rises in my chest. She's by the water fountains talking with Kirsha Turns and Jennifer Finkle, two supporting gypsies from the play—maybe the only three people in school who don't bust out laughing when they see me these days.

Still, I'm not dumb enough to believe I have a chance with Lani Andrews. But it's something in her eyes, how they light up with her smile. Maybe they do that for everyone, but they draw me in and make me stupid. They make me want to tell her the most impressive story anyone's ever heard. And not just that, it's how she's still the same girl I've always known. The kind of girl who will pluck a pineapple off your shirt without thinking twice about it.

Back in the fourth grade, Lani and I were paired together in Mrs. Wilmer's class for a science project. We did this ant farm thing, which doesn't sound like much, but Lani made it something amazing. She charted the ants' development, their work schedules, the effects of toxins in the dirt, their devotion to the queen. She even created a blog...about an ant farm!

We were sure to get an A on the thing, I mean Lani had poster boards, signs, charts, you name it. But then on the week of our presentation, we were unloading everything at the school, and guess what? Captain Clutts strikes again!

I dropped the farm on Mrs. Wilmer's desk. And by dropped, I mean tripped, fell, and the chucked the thing across the classroom. Dirt went everywhere—on the desks, spraying the walls, I think some even went down Mrs. Wilmer's blouse. Meanwhile ants skittered across the floor, and the entire class jumped up on their desks. Someone even screamed. By the time order was restored and the custodian swept up our project, everything was a bust.

I was crushed, destroying all of Lani's hard work like that. But she didn't even flinch. She did the presentation, even pointed to some of the escapees, and Mrs. Wilmer handed us a B+, which was not great for Lani but a step up in the world for me.

Now here we are seventh graders, and I'm still messing things up. Falling off stage or crawling on the football field or even flopping in the parking lot at the pizza place.

I need to get a grip. Because yeah, Lani is nice to me. But Lani Andrews is nice to everyone. Hoping for anything else is a waste of time.

I head for my locker, passing some cheerleaders. McKenzie Cooper's laughter follows me down the hallway. Think "cheerleader" and McKenzie Cooper appears out of a cloud of school spirit: pretty, blonde, and popular. But from what I could tell that was it. She's about as flimsy as one of those *Gypsies and Fairies* posters plastered down the halls.

If only Lani were unapproachable like McKenzie and the cheerleaders, I could get over myself and go stumbling off into the shadows. But Lani's smile has healing powers. It's sincere and dimply and dazzling and keeps me swimming upstream.

Moping down the hallway, I try to think of just one time when I didn't mess something up. Or maybe not mess something up in such a "Cluttstacular" way. The bell rattles, snatching me back to reality. I slog off towards gym class, past another poster for the latest New Faces production, thinking how the play should have been called *Gypsies and one really clumsy,   stupid-for-letting-himself-think-even-for-a-minute-that*

Lani Andrews-would-ever-even-consider-him-except-in-strictly-a-friend-kind-of-way boy. Not as catchy, but accurate.

What a mess. I bang my head against a locker, thinking about how I got myself into playing the fairy. It all happened so fast. One day, I'm headed to lunch, when I pass by Lani, busy recruiting for *Gypsies and Fairies*. She looked at me and smiled, and *boom*, I was hypnotized. I agreed to take the part. Now there's no going back.

Of course that role was vacant, because no guy in his right mind would take it. But again, around Lani I'm not exactly right-minded, which leaves me spending an hour before football practice crossing the asphalt sea with fairy wings and tights, on my way to the auditorium to rehearse my fairy spells. And each rehearsal only brings me one step closer to opening night, which Zach reminds me I will never, ever live down.

Chapter 5
By Default

I t's still crazy, walking through the heavy doors of Peakland High School towards the lobby, taking in the musty smells of sneakers and books, staring down the endless rows of lockers. I'm always tempted to sneak over to the trophy case, to the shrine dedicated to those great teams of Peakland past, but I'm too afraid to go roaming the halls alone, draped in fairy gear no less.

Entering the auditorium, I receive a standing ovation. The entire cast and crew drop everything and break into applause. My cheeks redden. I guess embarrassment is something you never grow out of.

"Well there he is, our famous sprite."

Can't say why he's calling me a drink. Mr. Worsham's got this funny accent I can't place. He's super tall and rail thin (think Abraham Lincoln, the vampire dude), always wearing a button down, tie, and his trusty blazer with the sleeves coming short of his wrists.

I take a seat on a trunk. "Sorry I'm late."

Truth is, I'm a little preoccupied with football practice. Without Trayvon or Ben it leaves me at the helm. But one problem at a time. For now, I have to deal with Worsham.

He offers a thin smile. "Mr. Clutts, your football video has sparked quite the buzz for our little production."

Some snickering from the stage crew. *So happy you could bring that up.* Mr. Worsham lets his little joke sit there on stage, dramatically. Lani says he used to be some big Broadway star. That he won a whole bunch of awards and junk and he's returned to his roots to give back. Now he's directing *Gypsies and Fairies*.

I nod and shrug, happy to oblige. Mainly because Preston Lockhart is staring at me like he owns the stage. Preston arrived at Peakland this year from some fancy private school across town. The guy's all about himself. In his khakis and sweaters, with his shaggy haircut that is actually a precise arrangement of layers. Preston's got a smile like a sword. It can flip from smirk to charming depending who's near. Not sure what the guy's future holds, but I'm guessing a bowtie and blazer is involved.

For now, Preston's landed the role of gypsy prince, which would be funny if I weren't playing a glitter-tossing fairy. And since the play centers around the gypsy prince marrying the gypsy princess—a' la, Lani, I'm not exactly in a position to laugh.

Truth is, Preston is a great actor—not that I'll ever admit it to his face—and where most of us are just biding our time, he and Lani seem to be taking the New Faces production seriously. It's pure torture watching them together, gypsy bride and groom. At least it's part of my role to ruin the wedding.

We take our places. And things aren't so bad. I manage to get through my lines and stay on my feet, even as Mr. Worsham positions me up closer to edge of the stage, right next to Lani, who touches my arm and smiles. "Steady there."

That's right, Lani touched my arm. Yay. So play rehearsal isn't so bad after all. The only thing left to do is survive football practice—a time usually spent doing homework or napping. But again, with our quarterbacks falling off the face of the earth, I just might be expected to play. Not yay.

Another trip across the parking lot, zig zagging between activity buses. Things are quiet at Peakland Middle except for the click of cleats down the hall. Sure enough, our little locker room is like a funeral parlor. No jokes, no laughs. Without Trayvon doing his standup routine, he and Phillip arguing about something stupid, it's just not the same. All heads are down, sullen stares. Not a smile to be found.

We all turn as Coach Jackson enters the room, Trayvon trails with a limp behind him. Someone gasps. Oh boy. Our quarterback is on crutches.

Coach Jackson's face is grim, even for Coach Jackson. His eyes are heavy, mouth tight. He holds a hand to his chin. I look around the room. This is not good. Not good at all.

Coach Barber falls in behind them, sniffling, wiping his puffy eyes as Coach Jackson takes the floor. "Okay guys, let's just get this out of the way." A quick glance to his son, hardly able to conceal his disappointment. "Trayvon had an accident on his skateboard. It appears he's broken his ankle."

Coach Barber muffles a sob, blows his nose. Because it also appears our season is over. Trayvon only stares at the floor. With our full attention, Coach Jackson turns to me, and the words I fear most fall right out of his mouth.

"Colt, get ready, you'll be taking reps with the first team today."

I nearly swallow my tongue. "*What?*"

The whole locker room deflates. Or maybe just Coach Barber. It doesn't exactly bolster my confidence.

Coach Jackson takes charge. "Okay, everyone just calm down," he says, sensing a mutiny, waving in the stragglers hanging back. "Come on, bring it back in guys."

The team takes a few cautious steps forward, exchanging worried glances. Coach fixes his cap. "We're two-and-one, and that's the good news."

Everyone is hunched over, picking their fingernails or fiddling with laces or helmet straps. We already know the bad news: the reason we're 2-1—Trayvon—has a big, bulky boot on his foot. Still, Coach Jackson continues on about how even with Trayvon out for the year, we can rally and overcome. It's nice and all, but he's lost us. Luke and Harrison shake their heads. I know what they're thinking, because I'm thinking it too.

The season is toast.

"Now, we have Ben and Colton. Only, I've been informed Ben has mono so he won't be back anytime soon. Sooo, Colton," he rolls a hand my way, "that leaves you."

Another collective sigh. The weight of every eyeball pressing on me nearly knocks me over. Coach Jackson is big on leadership and all, so when he nods to me I understand it's my turn to speak. I swallow the growing clump of nerves in my throat and attempt to rise to the occasion, but when I take the floor I accidentally kick over a helmet and it goes skidding into the locker with a clang. The team groans.

Coach Barber has his hat over his heart. I think he's humming TAPS. Coach Jackson wipes his forehead. I know he's wondering how we'll ever manage another first down with me under center. Phillip snorts as I pick up the helmet and try to tune it out. Slow and steady, I clear my throat and take the team by the reins, as my dad would say.

"Well, uh, I think, um, first, I uh, I'm sorry about that Trayvon."

Trayvon rolls his eyes. Nothing.

"Now, uh, we've got Jefferson this week and…"

"Hillsdale." Coach Jackson corrects. More snickering. A few guys drift back towards their lockers. Coach waves them back.

"Right, Hillsdale. But I think we can continue our winning streak. Right?"

Crickets.

The team groans and mumbles and I realize I'm not cut out for this. I should use this opportunity to tell Coach and everyone else that I'm retiring. But I already know Coach Jackson won't let me quit, and I can just hear my dad going on about fulfilling commitments and honoring obligations.

Instead, I try to suck it up and get some energy brewing. To find my voice and fake it till I make it. On television, sometimes before a big game, they show the team huddled and swaying in unison as one guy—a linebacker maybe—gets his team amped and ready for battle. Next man up and all. Only, that isn't happening here. Coach Jackson coughs.

"Okay," I say, cutting it short. "Let's get out there and have a great practice, Panthers on three. One, two, three..."

"Panthers," the team moans, as the vibe in the locker room flat-lines.

Because we are so dead.

Chapter 6
Assume the Position

Coach Jackson gives me a lift home, using the short ride for one of his thrilling pep talks. He hits the usual motivational points on the way. *You can do this. Don't overthink things. Just go out there and give it a hundred percent.* You know, typical coach speak. But it's kind of hard to take in with all of Trayvon's eye-rolling and snickering in the back seat.

Mondays at our house are Dad's night to cook. Mondays are also the night we're most likely to have a house fire. Sure enough, I find Dad in the kitchen, at the oven, and I have a sudden urge to check the batteries in the smoke detectors.

But first, the big news.

I plow ahead for the fridge. Abby glances up from her cards, where she's got a collection of vials and other nonsense scattered across the table. Never one to miss anything, she looks my way and her eyes fly open. "Wait. Did you actually play tonight?"

The bar is set pretty low when it comes to my football expectations. I give her a quick smile. Dad checks over his shoulder and glances at the dirt and grass stains on my football pants. "Hey, sport, look at you,"

Kind of funny, how my sister wears cloaks and hoods yet I'm the one who draws all the attention around here. I gulp down some Gatorade, thinking how I should play this. I mean, no reason to tell them my pants are stained because I got sacked seventeen times, that my legs feel like mush from running for my life, or that at one point I tossed eight straight interceptions until Coach gave me a "breather." Nope, better to tame expectations.

"Well, Trayvon broke his ankle and Ben has Mono, so by default you're looking at the new starting quarterback of the Peakland Middle football team."

Dad drops the spoon he's using to stir the sauce. It hits the floor with a clang, takes a high bounce—Clutts style—into the air to inflict maximum carnage. Sauce spatter hits the cabinets, the counters, I think some droplets make it to the ceiling, but those could have been flung last Monday. This, coincidently, is when Mom enters the kitchen.

"Hey what's going—" Her bag slips off her shoulder, like an anvil, to the floor. "Oh."

Abby smiles brightly. "Colt got promoted, we think."

Max comes panting around the corner to assist with the cleanup effort, joining Dad, who's on his knees, smearing sauce all over the cabinets.

"Yeah, he's starting at quarterback this week," Dad says in that funny voice, the high-pitched one he uses when Mom asks him if he likes her weird purse of the week. Her gaze roams to the oven door handle, where the fancy white towels Dad and I are never—ever!—supposed to use are missing. Oh boy.

"Rob." Mom swoops in with a roll of paper towels. Dad gets to his feet, finds the now orange towel in his hands, like it's a meteorite, then tosses the spoon towards the sink. He misses, spraying the counter with specks of sauce. Mom's head drops. I think sometimes she regrets the whole splitting kitchen duties thing. The other week, Dad torched a casserole so badly that the neighbors thought we were burning tires in the backyard.

But the mess is a good distraction. I've had enough attention today anyway. So with all the cleaning going on, I start to back away from the kitchen, but Dad catches me, all arms out and synergized—to borrow one of his office terms. "Colt, this is great. Now you can show Coach Jackson you've got what it takes."

Mom rinses the spoon at the sink and nods. And we all just stand around, all thinking the same thing: how epically bad can this get? Even Max, with sauce on his snout, sits quietly on the floor, his ice blue eyes fixed intently on my new pants.

The water hisses, boiling over. Dad whirls around but Abby leaps into action. "Here Dad, why don't you let me handle it?"

Mom turns to the sink, I think to avoid eye contact. "Well, that's great, Colt. First the play, now the football news."

Abby slides a card across the table, then jerks it back. "Wait, who are you guys playing this week?"

"Hillsdale?"

"Ouch." She sets a finger to her chin. "This is going to call for some protection spells for sure."

"Abby. No. It isn't."

Suddenly Dad looks pale. "Hmm. Hillsdale, you say?"

Everything stops. Even Max, his tongue hangs at mid swipe. Okay, so yeah, Hillsdale is a football factory. They haven't lost a game in years and their front line is bigger than the Dallas Cowboys. Am I afraid? No. I was afraid during football practice. This is a death sentence.

While I'm mulling this over, Abby moves to the sink. She breaks the silence, dumping spaghetti into the strainer. "Well, maybe this will help you out with Lani."

I set my best glare on my sister. Again with Lani. I've only mentioned it once to Abby, when she pressed me about my sudden interest in theater. And silly me, I thought that information was protected under the brother/sister confidentiality pact. I could kill her.

On cue, Mom sets the plates on the table and shoots me a wink. "Lani Andrews. She really is adorable, Colton."

Dad pipes up. "Lani, huh? You know, in high school, your mother and I—"

Abby and I both cover our ears to make it stop. *La la la la...* The only thing worse than Mom and Dad talking about my crush is Dad talking about him and Mom going out dancing, and —even worse—their first kiss.

Abby stops him short. "Dad. We know. We know way too much."

Mom, from the floor, says, "Remember that little science project?"

How my mom can remember this stuff is incredible. Unlike Dad, who's still lost in his memory, shaking his head. "Back in the day we actually went to dances."

Abby rushes to the window and checks the sky. "Okay, Colt. We have a new moon. Here's what you need to do. First, lie face down in the bathtub. Mom, do we still have the sea salt?"

Nope. No way. Abby's antics. Dad's memories. Lani. Dates. Curses. I need to escape my family. "Um. I'm going to go lie down for a minute. Face up. And not in a bathtub."

I get changed then collapse on my bed. I stare at the ceiling and try to dream up a scenario where this all turns out okay, but my thoughts tumble like my feet on the stage. The silence only makes it worse. It's no use, six minutes later I return to the kitchen where Mom has everything clean and restored. But Abby is still up to her tricks.

"You're going to have to let me help you."

Mom smiles at Abby. "Abby, we're trying to stay positive here." Then, to reinforce this positive moment they announce how Abby scored in the top percentile of her placement tests. Like, tops in the whole school. Again.

Abby looks at me and shrugs. Mom takes us in, beaming from across the table. "It seems both of you have had quite a week."

Dad drops his fork. I'm not sure what to think. Sure, I'm choking on my own breath about having to play against Hillsdale, but it's even worse how my own parents are terrified about it.

Mom turns to me, all gentle and pitiful. "Colton, listen, we are so proud of you, with the play and now this football thing. That being said, I just—"

"Guys, please. Can we just talk about something else?"

I don't mean to snap, but I have to stop Mom before she says it. There is no stupid curse, and I refuse to hear anything else about it. And it's then I notice Abby is wearing my fairy wings, adding some much-needed color to her wardrobe.

I set my fork down. "Abby, take off my fairy wings. And hey, that's my wand, too."

Abby glances up at Mom, who looks at Dad. All three of them—four if you count Max—are smirking. She wrinkles her nose at me. "Well, you left them on the floor, I didn't think you'd mind."

Mom sips water through a smile, composes herself, and says, "Abby, give the fairy wings and wand back to your brother."

I swear, it's so pointless. They're all cracking up so hard the table shakes. I remind them that the props are, you know, school property.

"That's right, Abby." Dad clears his throat, fighting off another laughing fit. "Hand your brother his school-issued fairy wings."

They lose it all over again. Abby makes a show of unhooking the wings and waving the wand in my direction. Then she digs in her pocket. "Here's your fairy dust." Her smile vanishes. "Oh, and I um, I might have made a few alterations."

"What? Abby, we aren't supposed to open that. Mr. Worsham will flip." I look to Mom and Dad, because their top-of-the-class brainiac daughter is tampering with school property and they don't even blink.

Abby slides the vial across the table. I hold it up to the light. It looks, well, like glitter. Brighter maybe, but glitter. I shake my head. "What did you do, Abby?"

She shrugs and gives Mom and Dad a darling little smile. "I just added a few things. It still needs one more—"

"No. It doesn't."

Mom reaches for my hand. "I'm sure it's fine, Colton. Eat your dinner, it's getting cold."

This family, I swear, you can do whatever you want just as long as you make honor roll.

Chapter 7
Glitter Litter

Zach and I hang in my basement Saturday night, playing video games and watching movies. If I thought it was bad after the *Fail* videos, he's been nearly unbearable since I told him I'd been named the starting quarterback. He paces, jacked up on Sour Patch Kids and Dr. Pepper, asking if I know what this means for us. *Us.* As though he's the one about to get clobbered.

By the fourth level of Alien Blasters, it's all he's talking about. How *we* should take advantage of *our* big promotion. His brainstorming is even enough to break his usual laser focus on the game, as he turns to me with an up-to-something grin. "You know, you should ask Lani if she wants to hang out," he says, still tapping away at his controller.

I pretend to be deep in concentration, even when he pauses the game, breaking our unspoken rule. He continues. "Come on, you're the quarterback now. We should ask her. I mean you of course, *you* should ask her, and maybe ask one of her friends, too. Maybe."

I know I shouldn't go along with him when he's like this. Then again, it's not like I haven't already thought about it a million and one times.

While Zach is hardly an athlete, he also doesn't have his own personal storm cloud hanging over his head. Still, he has to know that my "big breakout" is coming at a terrible time. Peakland Middle has *never* beaten Hillsdale Middle and

Hillsdale High has a ten-game winning streak against Peakland High. I mean, the last time Peakland beat Hillsdale, or "Killsdale" as they're known in these parts, our grandfathers were lacing up their cleats. Just thinking about it causes a trickle of sweat to fall from my armpits and drip down my ribcage.

I scoff and resume the game but fumble my controller, trying to play it cool. "Lani, you uh, you're talking about Lani Andrews, right?"

Zach laughs. He rolls his eyes, takes down a swig of Pepper without missing a button. "Dude, come on. Have you forgotten that I've known you forever? Is there another Lani who you stare at like a lost puppy? Then you get this goofy smile and your eyes kind of go all dazed whenever she walks by. Plus, you're in that fairy play with her so you've got an angle. Ask her."

If I'm hearing him right—which maybe I'm not because I'm still finding pizza cheese in my ear—Zach thinks I should march right up to Lani Andrews and ask her to, as he put it, "hang out sometime."

"Come, on. What do you have to lose?" he says without blinking, mashing buttons with practiced precision. "You need to pounce on your newfound popularity."

"My newfound—"

Before I can ask him where he gets this stuff, the doors to our space shuttle swoosh open and there stands the great Zorgob —the greenest, fangiest alien this side of the Milky Way. His sharp teeth drip and fizzle with alien spit, kind of how I imagine the Hillsdale linebackers will be licking their chops seeing me next week.

Zach starts blasting away, his fingers moving like lightning, in tune with his brain. Zach's thing is computers, video games, anything electronic. In the fifth grade he built this tube radio and brought it to school. It worked too, and we spent all of recess listening to Sports Talk.

But I don't want to "pounce" on any of it. Besides, Lani doesn't care about football or popularity. And not just that, I sort of like my low-pressure situation on the bench, with my helmet cooler and clean uniform. Sure, I know the offense backwards and forwards, all the formations and plays, but that doesn't mean I can *make* any plays on the field. Same for all this fairy drama stuff. I have my few lines down pat, but once that spotlight hits the stage, well—*crash*—like rehearsal.

It's too late, Zach has planted the seed in my brain. I spend the rest of the weekend considering the self-annihilating act of approaching Lani and, well, what? I have no idea. *Go to the park? Out for Ice Cream? A slice of pizza?* I don't know how these things work. The only good thing about all of this is Lani's the kind of girl who would let me down easy.

I'm no closer to knowing what to do on Monday morning when Zach hops off his front steps and checks the trashcan. Only I forgot to trash Abby's cards this time because I'm too preoccupied with worrying about the trash bag in my hands— the white bag that does little to hide the fairy wings and wand. I reach back and sure enough, find four Jacks.

Zach stops short and examines the bag of fairy props. "Dude. No."

"Look, I have to get this stuff out of my house. Abby keeps messing with it."

He nods along. "Yeah, don't you just hate it when your little sister gets into your fairy gear?"

"Ha ha. No seriously. I caught her doing some sort of spell with the fairy dust. It's weird."

Weird doesn't cover it. Last night I walked into Abby's room, ready to let her have it for taking my stuff again. I cracked the door, found her sitting on the floor, my wand in her hand.

She'd uncorked the vial of glitter and had all her stupid recipes out. Orange peel, bay leaves, clover, and whatever else she keeps in there. I opened my mouth and started to tell her to cut it out when, well, I know how this sounds crazy, but...the wings flapped.

It sort of freaked me out. So much I can't even tell my best friend about it. Now Zach stands there, grinning, just waiting. Finally, I shrug, ready to move on and get to school. "I just need to stuff this in my locker and be done with it."

"Whatever you say. So, have you thought about how you're going to do it?"

"Do what?"

"Duh. Lani? And a friend. Us? It's time we make our move."

I hold up the bag. "Sorry, I've been sort of busy. Haven't really thought about it."

He stops in his tracks and smiles. "Sure you haven't. Look, do you want to spend the rest of your life wondering why Lani ended up with freaking Prescott?" He breaks into a dance move that looks an awful lot like a guy trying to swat away imaginary pigeons raining from the sky. "Or do you want to show her what you've got."

"You're really bad at this."

Whatever boost of courage Zach supplied the other night hisses away like a flat bike tire. By the time we get to school, the fairy wings have poked a hole in the bag for all the world to see.

I speed walk the halls to my locker, where, after muffing my combination a couple of times, I stuff away the sparkly props. I edge them to the back with my history book, on top of a flattened brown bag that contains last week's ham sandwich. I turn to get going when I remember the vial of fairy dust. I toss the vial in and I'm about to slam the door when something flashes.

A quick look around. Then, leaning closer, the vial of glitter pulses, like a jar full of fireflies. I'm serious. I know how that sounds, but it's the only way to explain it. Besides, if you'd seen those wings flapping, well...anyway.

Holding my breath, I pick up the vial and give it a quick shake, wondering just what in the heck Abby did. It's not the lighting. The glitter pulses again, flashing brighter, drawing me in. I gently pop off the cork, leaning closer...closer still...

"Hey, Cold Cuts."

A shoulder crashes into my back. I fumble the uncorked vial into my locker and it's glitter city. Fairy dust goes up my nose, in my ears, everywhere. And still, even with my head inside the putrid confines of my locker, I recognize the squeaky laugh of my own personal cameraman. Phillip Jenkins.

I dislodge my head, sneezing like mad. It's like cinnamon, only worse. And not only did I get glitter up my nose, it's all over my shoes too. I quickly cap the vial and bury it in my pocket.

"What...*achew*...are you...*achew*...doing?"

Harrison stands behind Phillip, arms crossed and grinning.

"Look, it's the Epic Fairy Fail guy." Phillip reaches over me and snatches the wings, waving them around for everyone to see. It's Michelangelo's all over again. Only this time, instead of pizza sauce, it's glitter. "You wearing these to practice today?"

Laughter burns my ears. "No, they're just some props Mr. Worsham gave me to...hey!" I finally get my hands on the wings, but to my horror, Harrison has my wand.

"Man," he says, waving it around. "You've got to be kidding me."

He twirls the wand a few times over my head. Like a gift, the bell rings.

"Oh that's right, the play," Phillip says, looking to Harrison with a smirk. Harrison, tosses the wand back into my locker.

"Hey man," he says, backing away. "I don't care what you do

on your own time, but don't show up at practice wearing wings and glitter. It's not a good look. And you've got glitter all over your face."

Greenie, our fearless hall monitor, tells us to move it. The guy is roughly 114 years old and I'm not sure he's ever left Peakland Middle School. The rumor is he lives in the shed behind the woodshop. Either way, the guy's always around and looking for someone to bust. He hustles our way, breaking up the crowd. "Get moving, people. Get moving."

Harrison and Phillip start down the hallway, all head shaking and chuckling. I clean up the best I can, then slam my locker shut. I wipe my nose and dust off my shoes, then get going for class.

Chapter 8
Colt the Bolt

Here's the thing about glitter: once you get it on, you're not getting it off. It's like beach sand, how you find it in your shoes weeks after getting back from vacation. I spend the rest of the day sneezing out specks of gold and pink, still clueless on just how I'm going to ask Lani to hang out. Or whatever it is I'm supposed to ask her.

Surprisingly, Trayvon spends most of Earth Science giving me pointers about Hillsdale's defense. No matter, because I can't make any of the runs he can make so it's pretty much pointless to know the plays. I'm just happy he's talking to me, even if he does give me a hard time about the glitter. But overall he's in good spirits; the doctor says he'll be ready for basketball season. In the meantime, he's soaking up the sympathy like a champ.

At lunch I get exactly one bite into my turkey sandwich when Zach smiles real big, nudging Seth. "So Colt. Do you remember what we talked about?"

I wipe my hands on my lap. "I can't get this glitter off of me."

"You? Lani? A friend... *Ahem*, me?"

"Oh," I say, still wiping my sleeves. "Um, not really."

"Here's the plan," he begins, as though I never said a thing. He leans in low, his eyes darting around so everyone in the cafeteria can tell he's up to something. His breath smells like onion rings. "You're going to ask her if she wants to go to the lake."

I wipe at my forehead, trying telekinetically to urge Zach to drop it. He isn't picking up on his end though. He and Seth just stare at me.

"I uh, I'm not sure I want—"

"Come on, Colt. Just grow a pair. And put in a good word for me while you're there. I've been getting a vibe from Jennifer."

"A vibe? Right. Like that vibe you got from Allison last year?"

"Really? Still? Look, how was I supposed to know she had allergies? I still say she was winking at me. But trust me, this is different."

I take a quick peek over to Lani's table. She's sitting with some girls from the play. At the next table, just behind her back, lurks Preston Lockhart and his ilk.

Maybe it's food poisoning (Mom's been hitting up the markdowns on the lunchmeat as of late), or perhaps there's mold in the air ducts, but despite my fear, I feel my chair slide out from the table. I stand without losing my balance. Then, with Zach and Seth looking on with gleeful smiles, I lift my foot, gracefully I might add, and start for Lani's table.

I sidestep a chair sticking out in the aisle. It's weird, like I'm in slow-mo, even a soundtrack drumming away in my head and propelling me forward. Maybe Zach is right, I'm the quarterback now. And Lani *had* smiled at me the other day in rehearsals. Even touched my arm. With that, I take a trained breath. Fix my hair.

That's it, take it slow.

I cross the aisle into no-man's land. I'm completely exposed but doing okay. I stiff arm the little voice in my head, the one telling me *there's still time to break for the exit!* My nimble feet are doing the deciding now, bolstered by some unknown force that is determined to prove to Mom, Dad, Abby, and the whole family tree that I am not cursed.

A blur of faces. The hum of conversation is mere background noise to the throttle of my own heartbeat. Lani turns my way as I approach. No backing out now. Here goes.

"Uh, hide, Lani."

Hide, Lani? So much for being smooth. I am a first-class moron. "I mean, hi."

"Hey, Colt," Lani says, her smile inviting me to further butcher the English language. I try to block out Jennifer and Kirsha, and every other staring face.

"Hi." I say again, retooling my greeting. Lani blinks, still smiling. But that's tricky, she'll smile at anyone in the cafeteria, so it doesn't help me gauge whether I should proceed. Oddly enough, I do. "I uh, I'm... Hey, would you like to go to the lake sometime? Willow Park?"

Lake Willow, right up the road from the park. Perfect! Wow. Not bad. Go me. And my voice came out strong and without the nervous tremble I get when I'm on stage or talking to the entire football team.

Lani glances over to Jennifer and smiles. Then back to me. "Well, sure. But we have the play all next weekend, remember?" She tilts her head playfully.

Wait. Did she say sure, which I think means yes? I nod. "Oh, right. The play. Of course. Can't have the play without a fairy, right?"

"Nope. We sure can't." She laughs. It's a wonderful laugh, easy, pleasant, like a golden harp to my ears. But alarms are blaring in my head because Lani Andrews just said yes to the lake. I keep nodding, until I realize I look like a woodpecker.

"Well, um, see you at rehearsal."

"Yeah. Bye, Colton."

"Bye, Lani."

I slide away without a disaster striking. Riding high, I float back to our table, where Zach stares at me like I'm the baddest Alien Blaster this side of the Muratok Galaxy.

I slip into my seat, dazed. "She said yes. I think."

Zach looks across the cafeteria, then back to me. "Dude. You just did that."

I nod. He looks across again, then to me, shaking his head. "No, I mean. *You* just did that."

"I know."

"That was amazing. Nothing short of amazing."

"Right?"

"But um, dude, you really need to wipe the sparkles from your forehead."

I'm smiling so hard I can barely hear him.

And I'm still smiling in gym class, as we're playing basketball and Zach is still griping about how I didn't mention him to Lani. He shoots a brick and I chase down the ball and take a few dribbles. Maybe it's all the good vibes from my great day, but I'm feeling good. My whole body tingles. My legs feel kind of springy.

I spin off with two quick bounces between my legs as I come in for a lay-up. Only I'm light, super light, like gravity is more of a suggestion than law. I jump to go up, only I don't so much jump but catapult myself into the air. It's like at Jump Park, off the trampolines. Suddenly I'm like NBA-land high, soaring through the air, ball cocked back behind my head. I flush it down with two hands.

Hanging on the rim, I look down, past my dangling feet, trying to make sense of what's happened. Well, that and I have no idea how to get myself down. I've been trying to touch the backboard for most of the year, nicking it with my fingertip last week. Now I've just slam-dunked the ball like Lebron James on a breakaway.

Some wheezing below. Zach's face is frozen in disbelief as he stares up at me, arms limp and jaw gaping. He looks kind of small down there, with his argyle socks drooping over onto his Chuck Taylors. I use the net to lower myself until I can fall to safety.

"Dude. You just dunked." He's eyeing the rim like it's an alien spacecraft. I look back too, just to make sure it's still all the way up there. It is. Zach shakes his head. "You just, like," he makes a dunking motion, "dunked."

"I guess I did." I'm looking at my own palms like they're someone else's. I've only ever dunked a Nerf basketball goal that's hanging on my door. And even that was shaky.

Steve Kilmer and Dewayne Mills hustle over, shoes squeaking, matching shock on their faces. In my astonishment, I hadn't noticed that every ball in the gym has stopped bouncing. Everyone is staring at me.

"Do it again," Zach says, noticing the crowd.

"I don't know," I hear myself say, but my legs are shaking with energy. They feel like coiled springs. And while there's still glitter all over my socks and shoes, no one seems to care.

"Just try." He tosses me the ball and turns on the Zach charm, going all Barnham and Bailey, arms waving as he whips up the audience. *Step right up, step right up!*

A few quick dribbles and I wipe the soles of my shoes for traction. "This is crazy," I whisper to myself, right before I go up and slam it home again, this time a backward, two-hand jam that gets the whole gym oohing.

Coach Glover comes waddling out of his office near the locker room, still chewing on his lunch and wiping his mouth with a napkin. "Whoa, Colt. I didn't know you had hops."

I don't. At least, I didn't. But for the rest of gym class I'm doing things I've only seen on video games. Like a three-sixty, through the legs windmill, then I jump over some hurdles Zach sets up in front of the goal. I do so many gravity defying dunks my wrists are marked red and sore from the rim. The rim! Because I, Colton Clutts, can suddenly dunk a basketball. That's right, Fairy Boy has the whole gym waiting for his autograph.

Coach practically begs me to come out for the basketball team. He says I don't even need to try out. I'm on the team.

Everyone slaps my back. All order is forgotten. Usually Zach and I spend the time waiting for the bell talking about video games or whatever, but instead we're swarmed by the entire gym class. I look up to the basketball goal, wondering when I'm going to wake up.

But I'm wide awake. I'm as awake as I've ever been. And just like that, *Colt the Bolt* is born.

Chapter 9
Playtime

Word spreads quickly about the dunks, half the basketball team surrounds me in the hallway like I'm already on the team. They ask about my moves, my training, where I play AAU ball. By the time I get to my locker, grab my wings, wand, and glitter and book it across the lot to Peakland High, I'm ten minutes late for play rehearsal.

Mr. Worsham cranes his head as I rush into the auditorium. "Well, Mr. Clutts, so glad you could make it."

And get this, I'm not even frazzled when all heads turn my way. Instead I glide down the aisle with ease. I even smile. "Thanks, me too."

I leap onto the stage to muffled giggles and whispers. I can't help noticing Lani, in a dress and flowery crown, looking like the prettiest gypsy in the forest. She said yes to the lake, you know.

Mr. Worsham claps his hands. "Well okay, now that our fairy has arrived, let's begin." He motions to our places. "Okay, let's take it from the scene in the forest."

Lani takes her place at the trees, where she stands beside Preston, her husband-to-be. This is where the fairy—me—spies on the two gypsy lovers. Like I said, *Gypsies and Fairies* isn't Shakespeare.

Preston sidles up to Lani, his voice clear and powerful and stupid. "Well, my love, we are to be married tomorrow."

Maybe it's a carryover from gym class. From lunch. But I'm

still tingly and seeing Preston and Lani onstage is driving me crazy, because they do sort of look like a couple. So I take matters into my own wand, improvising, waving it behind Preston's head.

Lani snorts when she sees it. The other gypsies lose it too.

"What?" Preston says, breaking character, looking around, checking himself over and making sure he's tied and buttoned. I duck behind a wooden tree then peek out again, making a face. The entire cast loses it.

Mr. Worsham calls things to order. "Okay, let's give it another shot, and umm, Mr. Fairy, try to stick to the script, please."

"Sorry."

It takes a few minutes for the cast to pull it together. No one really takes this thing all that seriously. Well, almost no one, Preston is glaring at me, maroon with anger. But it's the most fun I've had since coming out for the play.

After rehearsal, I catch up with Lani and walk with her out to the parking lot where the sun has dipped behind the row of pine trees. The activity buses idle at the curb, some teachers linger near their cars, trading war stories and probably all the gossip we're not supposed to hear.

Lani zips up her fleece. "So I heard about Trayvon. That's too bad, huh?"

"Yeah, I'm not sure the team is so happy about it."

"What about you? It's your big chance."

I shrug. "Well, I don't know..."

Lani smiles. "If it's like gym class, you should be fine."

"Oh, you heard about that?" No big deal and all. I smile, walking backwards with no trouble at all. I even hop over a small branch on the sidewalk. No small feat for a Clutts. I don't know what it is, but I sure don't feel like me. I feel, well, almost super.

Lani's eyebrows rise with her smile. "*Everyone* is talking about it."

"Yeah, well, Zach's got a big mouth."

She scans the lot, the wind breezing through her hair. I watch her until I realize I'm staring, but then she looks at me and smiles. "I didn't know you were such a comedian. At rehearsals and all."

"Oh, well, it was kind of boring in there, just trying to liven things up."

Her face drops, and I feel bad for saying it. Theater isn't boring to her. Before I can apologize, she gives me a smirk. "I thought you livened things up last week," she says just as my phone beeps. A text from Zach.

U R the man!!!

A van pulls up to the curb. It's filled to the windows with what looks like coats, scarves. Winter clothes. "What's up with the coats?"

Lani's mom waves to me. I wave back. Lani starts for the van. "Oh, we're doing a coat drive at the Salvation Army. You have any winter garments you'd like to donate?"

"Uh, I can check and see. Hey, I didn't mean that, about..."

She gives me a smile that sends my feet shuffling. "Great. Whatever you can spare. See you tomorrow. Good luck at football practice."

I smile back, thinking about how the last time I saw her van I was swimming in pizza. How everyone was gushing about my flop. But now, turning for the football field, Lani waving from the window, things couldn't be much better.

IF I THOUGHT theater was boring, it's nothing compared to football practice. Coach Jackson has me hand off to Luke a million times. Obviously, without Trayvon, our playbook is limited. Then again, *with* Trayvon our plays were limited. I mean, the guy is so good he usually blows by everyone for a touchdown. Besides, this is middle school, we don't exactly pass the ball a whole lot.

Coach Barber is still sulking, even as Coach Jackson goes through the whole next-man-up spiel. The big guy is mourning his star. Again, where Coach Jackson is all defense and field position, Coach Barber only knows offense. And our offense is parked on the sidelines with a boot on his foot.

We're halfway through practice when Coach Jackson leaves the field to meet with a parent. And I guess Coach Barber just can't help himself. He tells Luke to take a breather and calls a pass play. Oh boy.

The call is a simple screen pass. A quick dump off to the running back. But lining up, it's like gym class all over again. I feel like it's time to show them a little something.

Hike. I drop back and fake the screen to Luke. Just as soon as I do, Harrison, our speedy wide receiver breaks downfield. I zip a laser pass and hit him in stride. Everyone turns to me. Mouthpieces leap from mouths. I only shrug.

Coach Barber rushes the field, his jiggly face smiling with joy. "Whoa boy," he says, yanking up his shorts. "Colton, where did that come from?"

Another shrug, a smile curling at my lips.

"That ball had smoke coming off the laces. Run it again. Hey yo, Coach J, come take a look at this."

We line up to run the play again. The play the defense already knows is coming. Doesn't matter. The ball finds my hands and I scamper around the pocket, pump fake, then launch a low, steaming spiral thirty yards to Harrison. It's on the money, but he drops the ball and shakes his hand.

"Dude."

"Sorry."

Trayvon perks up. The guys on the sidelines inch closer to the field. From there, we score quickly and score often. Harrison is all smiles now that he's getting the ball, and together we take the offense right down the field. I'm flinging passes left and right, and I even spin off a linebacker and skate twenty yards for a touchdown.

Trayvon is bouncing up and down on his crutches, and by the time Coach Jackson has us take five, the whole team is hyped up, including Coach Barber, who's talking like he's been sucking on helium. I can't help but notice how he's sort of taking credit for my sudden turnaround. "I knew it, I knew if I just coached him up some..."

Coach Jackson fixes his hat, still scowling. "Colt, where did this come from?"

Some track walkers have gathered to watch the show. Just like gym class I shake my head and laugh. "Honestly, I don't know, Coach."

"Okay, here we go." Coach Barber drags out a tackling dummy. He has the guys set it fifty yards away. Coach Barber blows the whistle. "Colt," he pants, giddy as a kid at Christmas. "Let her rip."

I drop back in my own end zone, cock the ball, and strike. The ball leaves my hand like a heat-seeking missile. It hits the dummy and the thing explodes. The vinyl splits and the padding splays out at midfield. The whole team goes quiet. Finally, Coach Jackson removes his hat and wipes his forehead. "All right, save some for Hillsdale."

No words. I look at my own hand, my arm, still cheesing hardcore. And since everyone's already heard about gym class, Phillip and Harrison have nothing to say about the fairy props in my locker this morning. And yeah, Phillip has his phone out, but this time to capture what has just happened. Some of the guys and Coach Barber rush off to the debris to take pictures of the dead tackling dummy.

I can't wait to get home and tell Mom and Dad about this. *Oh really guys, a curse huh? Ha.* I'll throw this stupid curse talk right in their faces, let them try to explain how I've asked Lani out, become a gym class legend, *and* a football hero all in one single school day.

And that's when it hits me like a linebacker. I glance down to the glitter on my shoes. I think back to Abby's room, the wings flapping. Her spells and potions and gibberish.

But...

Slam dunks. Perfect passes. Me, walking calm and cool across the cafeteria. No, there's no way. Of all the explanations it's the most far-fetched and the most logical answer of all. But no. There is no way one of my sister's stupid spells actually worked.

Is there?

Chapter 10
Research

I'm not saying Abby is a real witch, but I need some real answers here. Like, what exactly did she do to the glitter? Is it the glitter at all? Can a middle-schooler play in the NFL?

But things are getting weird at home, too. Luckily, Dad is too distracted with a meeting and Mom is busy handling a house closing so no one asks about my day. Even as Abby smirks her way through dinner, oddly wearing a green shirt instead of her customary black. It must be laundry day, only her hair is different, too.

I'm too drained, my brain too fried, to ask—to give her the satisfaction—about whatever is going on. I need to do some troubleshooting. So I pretend everything is ho-hum. Nothing to see here.

The next day I don't touch the vial. I keep it corked and take a shower and wear clean clothes so I'm completely glitter free.

Sure enough, I get to school, and when I see Lani in the hallway I nearly take out the water fountain. My shoes are cast iron and my underarms a swampland. I nearly double over with panic.

"Hide Colt."

"What, why?"

She giggles. "Oh, the other day, remember?"

Her eyes dance with her smile. She's got her hair pulled back except for one little twirly strand falling past her cheek. I steady myself at the window. Lani tilts her head and gives me a funny look.

"You okay there, Colt?"

I need to speak. Form real words and not gibberish. But my mouth is dry and my voice breaks. It's all wrong. Where I felt so cool and collected yesterday I'm now a mess of nerves. Only the first bell saves me from further humiliation. I manage to churn out a few sounds that pass as words.

"Yeah, I just, I gotta go."

"Okay," she says with a smirk. "Goodbye."

I scuffle up the hallway and around the corner, dashing for the bathroom, but I manage to trip over the cluster of kids sitting on the floor. Faceplant.

"Nice form, dude."

No time for jokes, I get back on my feet, slipping and sliding without traction. Once I'm in the bathroom, I splash cold water over my face.

Unbelievable. I'm right back to being me.

Abby. Impossible. But what else could it be? My transformation and now back again. I need to find her. Because more than anything else—more than swallowing my pride and admitting she was right—I'm going to need more glitter. Maybe even another spell. But first and most importantly, I need to get through the morning.

Being a sixth grader, Abby and I have different lunches. And so, I come up with a cough, procure a hall pass, and set off for the cafeteria. I slink past classrooms and stop by my locker where I ease the door open, not wanting to have to explain why I'm roaming.

There it is, sitting empty on top of my Earth Science book. Only a few grains of sand and grit. I shake what's left and... nothing. My heart picks up a beat. I tilt the vial back and forth, wondering if yesterday really happened. I uncork it. I swipe yesterday's spillage off my book and carefully get it back into the vial. It's painstaking work that takes a steady hand. Only I have two shaky hands. And it's no use. Nothing's glowing, just a bunch of sand. No glow, no go.

Then I hear some shuffling behind me.

"Okay, what was that?"

I stuff the cork back on the vial, slam my locker, and spin around. Preston Lockhart, his cocky grin stretched wide.

"Nope, I'm uh…" I've got nothing.

Preston straightens his back, jutting out his chin like he's onstage. "Are you tampering with the props? It's school property you know."

This guy. Seriously. I roll my eyes. "Look Preston, I don't have time for this."

"Yeah?" He nods towards my locker. "What, did you use up all your glitter? From what I can tell you've really been getting in touch with your inner fairy."

"That's it," I manage with a big gulp of a swallow. "You got me. I'm just trying to get into character."

He scoffs. "Yeah, okay Colton. I know you're up to something."

His message sent, Preston spins off and heads wherever it is he's going.

When he's gone, I suck down a breath and crack open my locker again. Even with a hall pass, I don't have much time. I swoosh down the hall, past several classroom lessons, headed for the cafeteria.

Abby is nowhere to be found. Only loud sixth graders chewing with their mouths open. Then I realize my mistake. I'm looking for a girl sitting alone, cloaked in black and reading Harry Potter. Instead I find Abby wearing a pink shirt. Pink! And I'm floored to see her laughing with other girls. My sister has friends. The world as I know it has turned upside down.

It's her all right, wearing normal clothes, sitting at a table in the middle of a group of girls, chewing and talking and laughing and being otherwise normal. I stand at the doorway, hoping she'll see me. She doesn't. And so I not so stealthily slide past the monitors and walk up to the table, where five or six little heads swivel around and look up at me.

"Colt, what are you doing here?"

Abby's friends (a whole table full of them) all turn with metallic smiles. I nod and ask Abby to step out to the hall. I need to talk to her. And that's when Greenie comes up behind me. "What are you doing in here, Clutts?"

"Uh, family emergency. I need to talk to my sister."

A redheaded girl turns to Abby. "Colt's your brother?"

Abby narrows her eyes at me. "Emergency?"

"Two minutes," Greenie grumbles. He motions to Abby, who reluctantly slides out and tells her "friends" she'll be right back. I look them over again. Seriously, who knew she had friends?

"What in the world?"

"The glitter. It worked."

A smile breaks across her face. "*What?*"

"The vial. The spell. Whatever you did, it worked." I look over her shoulder. "Did you put a spell on them too? I didn't know you had friends."

"Shut up," she snaps, but her eyes are wide with surprise. Then she squeals. "Really? It worked? Yes!"

I take a quick look over my shoulder, lower my voice. "Yes, it worked. Now I need you to do it again."

She takes a step back and shakes her head in such a Mom-like way that I almost expect her to lecture me on skipping class. "Um, I don't think so, Colt. I'm sort of over it. Hey, why aren't you in class?"

"Wait, wait. Hold on. *Over it?* Like, over being a witch? Oh, no. You cast a spell and *it works*. And now you're over it? I don't think so."

"Colt. I'm sure it didn't work. I don't even know what I did."

My voice deepens with urgency. "Abby. Listen to me. I'm slam dunking basketballs and scoring touchdowns. Do you really need more proof? Help me out. Please. I really need more of this stuff. Like soon."

She grimaces. "Hmm, that is strange."

"Figure it out. Tonight. Okay?"

"No way, I have plans."

"Plans? You're in the sixth grade."

Abby looks back in the cafeteria. Then turns back to me with a smirk I've come to recognize.

"What?"

She cocks her head. She's in the driver's seat and knows it. "Say it."

"Say what?" I sigh. In the cafeteria, Greenie's looking impatient, checking his old Casio like it's a Fitbit.

Abby twirls. She runs her fingers over the lockers, really enjoying my misery. "Oh, I don't know. That I was right. That you were wrong. That I was—"

"Okay, okay," I say too loudly. Then, lowering my voice, "You were right. I was wrong."

Abby's grin spreads like wildfire. She sets a hand to her ear. "I'm sorry, what's that big bro? I didn't hear you."

"Abby, come on. You were right, okay?" Greenie taps his watch and starts huffing our way. Abby tilts her head.

"My room. Seven fifteen. You get ten minutes."

Greenie starts for us but has to stop to pick up a banana peel. I turn to Abby. "I'm on a schedule, now?"

"Take it or leave it."

I can't believe this. "Fine."

Greenie comes clomping out. He's wiping at his shirt. His

comb-over looks like it's been through a windstorm, his pants in a bunch. He's got a big ketchup stain on his beige shirt. "Okay, people. Break it up. Clutts, back to class."

With a smirk, Abby spins and heads back to her table. I turn to go back to class, wondering what I'm supposed to tell Coach. Because without the glitter, I surely can't go to practice.

AFTER DINNER, Abby and I get to work. We have to be careful though, Mom already suspects something's up after we didn't fight or bicker at the table before we had to go hurry off to "study" after dinner.

Once in her room, I hand her the vial. She looks it over. "Hmm."

I roll my eyes. For nearly a year she's been Sabrina, clad in black and riding brooms. Now, she sits in front of me, bobbing to a Selena Gomez song and frowning at the vial. The same vial just two days ago she mixed and matched and stumbled upon a spell.

I try to coax her along. "Just do whatever you did before."

She looks at me like I'm dense. Spread out on her floor is her composition book—filled with scrawls and sketches. "Yeah, easier said than done. I think I used mustard seed, but," she flips a page, "wheat grass?"

I sit back, tossing a football in my hands. "Abby, you should have seen it. I mean, I decapitated a tackling dummy."

Speaking of practice, I had to tell Coach Jackson I wasn't feeling too hot. With mono going around he took me seriously and agreed to let me skip. Only two days until Hillsdale and he wants me rested and ready.

She looks up, confused. "You did *what?*"

I shake my head. Abby's walls are still covered in X-Men

wrap from when she'd been in that stage. It seems like years ago when Mom and Dad had taken on that project. Dad tumbled off the ladder and nearly out of her window. Then came Halloween, and she's been witchy ever since. Now she's become —I look her over—I don't know, way too normal. And annoying.

"Seriously, Abby. This is like, life and death. What did you put in my glitter?"

She shakes her head. Ignoring me. "Oh, here it is. Sea salt. Food coloring."

"No, what else?"

"I don't know. I just..." And then her eyes flash. "Hey, where's the wand?"

"In my locker."

Her shoulders slump. She shakes her head at me. "Idiot."

Again. Only weeks ago I was her idol. Now I'm an idiot. But I have to take it easy on her. If she can't replicate the spell, I'll get chewed up worse than a Nerf football in Max's paws. "How was I supposed to know you needed the wand? What exactly were the ingredients?"

"I told you, I'm not sure. Okay, let me think. Sea salt. Food coloring. And just, this spell I sort of made up. I was only trying to help, with Hillsdale and all I didn't want you to get killed. You know, they're really big and you're not that—"

I wave my hands to shush her. "Okay, okay, we're getting off track. Focus."

"Focus. Focus. Focus." Then she giggles, like the old Abby again. "Ha. Hocus Pocus. *Focus.* Get it?"

"No."

She flips through the book. Card tricks, what looks like a maze. Constellations and, is that an equation? Nerd alert. I'm getting frustrated, about to leap up and storm out and tell her she's the worst witch I've ever met, when suddenly she stops, and I can practically feel the light bulb pop on.

She hops up with the book and smiles. "Wait. Here it is."

I could hug her I'm so happy. She gives me that new Abby smirk, the know-it-all smirk. Then she reminds me again. "I'm going to need the wand."

"Done."

Chapter 11
Two Days Later

Gameday. I stroll into the school. No slips, no trips, no jitters or spills. I'm all swagger and smooth as I enter the lobby where the cheerleaders hung a *Go Peakland, beat Hillsdale!* banner above the main hallway. My chest swells as I spot my name, just under the *Go*, spelled out in curly swirly girl handwriting. Being the quarterback has its perks.

Abby worked her magic. I scored some craft store glitter and she did the rest. Only this time there's a slight hitch to the spell, one that she swears was not intentional. It seems I have to be wearing at least one other prop with the glitter in order for it to work. As in glitter and wand. Glitter and wings. Glitter and, yep, tights. Again, Abby says it was an honest mix up. I have serious doubts about that.

I go with the tights. And it works, the last few days have been something. I don't know what exactly or how exactly, but with her spells and my urging, we cooked up a batch of glittery goodness. *Use sparingly*, she advised. *And keep it corked, dork.* Blah, blah. Whatever. Super-stardom awaits.

McKenzie and the cheerleaders see me and come running. They've seen what I've been doing at practice, in gym class, and now they're all ribbons and pom poms and big bubbly smiles. They stop and break out into a personalized cheer.

Ready? Okay!

Run Dash, Score, Bolt

Who's our quarterback? His name is Colt!

I can think of worse ways to start a school day. And even more amazing is that my pulse remains calm and collected. No swampland armpits for me, my ecosystem is dry and cool. The cheer ends with a flurry of kicks and screams, and I bow and offer my applause. "Why thank you, ladies."

When they crank up another cheer, I find Lani, hanging back with a smirk. I shrug and she steps forward. Her hair is pulled back and her eyes sparkle behind her glasses as she watches the cheerleaders do cartwheels down the hall. "Well, you sure know how to make an entrance."

I'm still playing it cool, at least until the fairy wings pop out of my locker. "Oh, um, man these things won't stay put."

"Oh, that's right," she says, reaching for them. "I almost forgot that you were in our play."

All I can do is hang my head. I've skipped the past two rehearsals because Coach Barber has expanded the arsenal, as he calls it, drawing up some new emergency offensive plays for Hillsdale.

Lani folds up the wings and sets them neatly on my books, wrinkling her nose. "You might want to clean out your—"

Before she can finish, the cheerleaders tumble back to us again with another uh, cheer.

Colt...Colt...Colt...Beat those dolts!!!

"Okay," Lani laughs, starting off down the hall. "I'll talk to you later." She turns and walks backwards, hands cupped at her mouth. "Take good care of those wings! Mr. Worsham won't be happy if you bend them."

I'm grinning like a dork as I shut the wings with the wand in the locker, stuffing the vial of glitter in my pocket for safe keeping. But when I turn around I see Trayvon watching me, his arms draped over the crutches, confusion all over his face as he watches his former back-up—back-up to his back-up, even—

soaking up all the attention from the cheerleaders who used to parade him to class every day.

And what can I say? I nod my chin, but he just shakes his head and hobbles down the hallway.

McKenzie shoots me a wink and the cheerleaders are off, leaping and springing down the hallway. I stand with my back to my locker, in a daze. At least until Zach runs up to me, breathing hard with a goofy smile. "Major alert dude, I think McKenzie Cooper is into you."

"Really?" I look back at the girls as they hop and bounce and do their best to conjure up some school spirit at 8:03 am.

"Oh, yeah."

Zach places a finger to his chin and scrunches up his face like he's pondering something. "Man, what a problem you have on your hands. Lani or McKenzie? Such a tough dilemma. But you can introduce McKenzie to me if you'd like?"

"Yeah," I say, shoving him off, but thinking about this new "dilemma." It sure beats the old problems, I'm thinking, as I pat the vial in my pocket.

You've got to love having a witch for a sister.

Chapter 12
Pregame

I blow off play rehearsal yet again to rest up for my game. After three heaping bowls of Cap'n Crunch I'm on the couch, dreaming of glory, zipping passes left and right, the crowd goes wild, shaking me, shaking me. Shaking me into the real world.

"Dude, uh, what are you doing?" Zach stands over me, his arms stretched out.

"What time is it?" I ask through a yawn. Zach swipes my legs off the couch.

"It's almost five. I can't believe you actually fell asleep. Today of all days. Seriously, what's going on with you?"

I stretch out, wiping sleepies from my eyes. "I'm hungry."

The next thing I know, Zach is yanking at his hair, pacing from one end of the room then back. "Look man, I've known you for what, three and a half years now. And no offense, but you're the clumsiest, bumbling, most high-strung guy I've ever met. You're not even allowed to have caffeine after lunch because you get all cranked up and jittery."

I sit up and rub my face. "Is this some sort of pep talk?"

"And now," he says, ignoring me. "All of a sudden you don't even think twice. You just roll up and ask Lani Andrews out?" He starts counting off his fingers. "You've got your own personal cheerleading squad at school. You're leaping out of the gym and killing it at football practice? On top of all that you're...*sleeping* before the biggest game of your life? And um, dude? You're wearing purple fairy tights. I mean, bruh, don't get me wrong. I don't judge. But you gotta fill me in here."

Max hops off the couch with a jingly shake of the collar. I can't blame him for seeking a more peaceful place to nap. I take a deep breath and study my best friend. It takes a lot to get Zach riled up, but once he's there, he's there. His face is balled up and his eyes are squinty, like when he's really concentrating on Alien Blasters.

But he's right. He's been with me since day one, through it all. Sure, he gave me some stuff about falling off the stage, but he's always had my back. Always. If I can't trust him, I can't trust anyone.

I wipe my hands on my lap. "Okay, you really want to know?"

He stops and stares me down, eyes wide like it's the dumbest question he's ever heard. I swing my legs out and stand. "Well, okay, you know the play, right? All those props?"

"Yeah," Zach says, throwing his hands up. "What does that have to do with..." he stops, looks at the tights.

"Well," another big breath. "Remember how Abby kept messing with everything?"

He nods. It's all so outrageous. Nothing left to do but spill it. I start with Abby clowning around with the wand and the vial and then the glow of the glitter. About her actually getting a spell right.

Zach runs his hands through his hair. Like he's getting worried about me. "Um, dude. I love you like a brother and all, but I think you might need to lay off the—" I pull out the glitter while he's talking, "OKAY WHAT IS THAT?"

The vial pulses to life. His eyes go wide but then he shakes it off and shrugs. "So, you like, put glow worms in there."

I shake my head. My voice falls to a whisper. "Zach, she did it."

"Did what?"

He knows what, though. And this is why Zach's my man. Because he doesn't run out the front door screaming how I'm out of my mind. Instead he gives me that same devilish smile he'd given me when he snuck stink bombs into summer camp.

"You're kidding," he says, inching closer. I hand him the vial. The glow peters out. Just sand. Zach's smile falls. He holds it up closer. "What happened?"

"I don't know. Maybe it only works for me. But those dunks? The other day at practice? That was the day I spilled it all over me. It was the glitter, Zach."

He hands the vial back and it comes to life again. Zach's eyes flash, more smiling. I hand it to him again, and again the glitter goes dark. He holds it to the window so it catches the sunlight. Nothing magical is happening.

"Can I, uh, could I try some?"

"Well, there is a catch."

I tell him about the props. He brushes me off. "Come on, let me give it a try."

I figure now that Abby knows the recipe, what's the harm? It never hurts to try. "Okay." I pop the cork. "Give me your shoes."

"I'm uh, not wearing socks."

Great. Zach rips off a sneaker and immediately things become supremely unpleasant. Max comes prancing back in the living room, nose in high gear because he has a fondness for all things putrid. I shake some, turn my head for a breath and then do the other shoe. "Let's see how that works."

I go get dressed for the game. When I return, Max is going berserk, barking and howling like he did when he saw the mailman. Zach is trying to jump up and touch the ceiling. He's about two feet short.

"See? It only works when I'm wearing tights."

"You're serious?"

"Yeah, or wings, I guess."

"This is crap," he says, huffing and out of breath. Then, like I'm watching the wheels in his brain turn. "I need my own glitter. Where's Abby?"

"I don't know," I shrug. "She's out with friends, I think."

He cocks an eyebrow. "Abby has friends?"

"Yep. She even went to a sleepover the other night. Oh, and she's wearing pink now. I think she's finally moving out of her Goth stage."

He takes another swipe at the ceiling. Not even close. I pocket the vial and start for the door. Zach looks down to his feet, shaking his head. Then he says what I've been thinking for a couple days now. "Man, this is a bad time for Abby to quit being a witch."

"Yeah."

We're quiet for a minute. Only the wheeze of Zach's heavy breaths fill the room. "Okay so...I want to see what happens."

"What happens?"

"You know. The glitter. With you."

With a shrug, I pop off my shoes, wiggle my toes. Zach snaps his fingers. "Hey, maybe if I wore your tights?"

I shoot him a look. "I don't think so."

Honestly though, I don't know the details, but there's no time for theories right now. If ever I needed some fairy magic, today's the day. With nothing to lose, I pop the cork and shake some into my yard-sale cleat.

A pinkish glow. My old shoe sparkles as a glittery swirl rises over our heads. Max backs away with a growl. Zach reaches out, trying to get a handful of magic.

"Whoa."

It's like Abby added some pop to this batch. I even let go of the shoe and it hovers in front of me in a pinkish cloud. Zach takes a step back, his face completely still. "Dude, I think I just peed my pants."

My own breaths are short and shaky as I slide my foot in. Bam. My foot starts tapping, restless and bouncing. I nearly hop right out the door on one foot.

But I have to hurry. It's almost kickoff so I dab some into the other cleat. More swirly magic. More twinkling. Way more tapping. This time when I stand I have to hold on.

I look at Zach and smile. "Let's do this."

CLICKING and clacking along the sidewalk, my legs are like springs. Hopefully no one's watching us because Zach is kind of hopping along, staring at my legs. "How does it feel?"

I shake my head, my legs itching to move. "I'm guessing it's what a racehorse feels like in the gates before the Derby."

With Hillsdale in town, there are actually cars in the parking lot. I zip down to our little field, where the cheerleaders are revving up the crowd filling up the bleachers. Sweet, I'm ready to put on a show.

Coach Barber nearly tackles me. The rest of the guys are clowning around, some with headphones on as they go through their own pregame ritual. My own pregame until this point was deciding what kind of gum I was going to chew while I rode the bench. But today is different. Way different. And after what I've been doing in practice, I think the team is convinced we have a chance to break this losing streak.

But old habits are hard to break. Phillip scoffs, pointing at my legs. "Nice tights."

Let them laugh. They'll see. Even if a part of me, buried deep under my shoulder pads, beneath the giant grin on my face, is kinda/sorta, absolutely terrified.

Coach Jackson calls us over to one end of the field. With his all-business approach he stalks along beneath the goalpost, working over something in his head. He seems more uptight than usual without Trayvon playing. And who can blame him for that?

McKenzie and the cheerleaders roll out the Panthers banner, ready to greet us when we storm the field. But first, Coach Jackson grumbles into his speech. He begins by stating the obvious. "Okay guys, somebody will come out of this with a loss."

I'm tempted to raise my hand and remind him that a tie is possible, but this doesn't seem like the time.

He continues. "We have to want it more. We have to earn it."

This goes on for a while, the motivational stuff he must have picked up at an offseason workshop or something. I glance around the huddle. Big Chris Clover, our defensive lineman, looks ready to rip the bumper off a Toyota. Luke bobs his head with a serious game-day glare in his eyes. Harrison too, is all business.

It occurs to me that maybe I used too much glitter, because I can *feel* the magic climbing through my limbs, chasing off the fluttery nerves and doubt. Rushing over the fear. In fact, with Coach going on about who wants it more, I'm getting a little bored. What I *really* want to do is get out there and do my thing.

After an eternity, Coach rambles ahead to a dramatic close. "Okay guys, bring it in. Panthers on three."

We rip through the banner and take the field. For a middle school football game, this is as big as it gets. Hillsdale has traveled well, packing in fans on the visitor side. The smell of popcorn is in the air. I turn and spot Mom and Dad in the bleachers as Harrison and Luke strut out for the coin toss.

Coach Jackson calls me over. "How you doing, Clutts?"

I nod. "Good, Coach." *You'll see.*

He gives me a fierce linebacker stare. "Okay, well, just do like you've been doing at practice and we should be okay. If you get rattled, call timeout. Got it?"

"Yes, sir."

Chapter 13
Showtime

We elect to receive. After the opening kick, I lead the offense out onto the field—gracefully, I might add—and take the huddle.

"So, what do you guys think? Should we snap this losing streak?"

A few chuckles, someone asks about my backside, and then there's the whole thing about my tights. I shake it off, knowing my killer practices have won most of them over. I call Coach's play and we break from the huddle.

Lining up, I check out the defense. Yep, Hillsdale is just as big and nasty as advertised. They look ready to mangle me with nine in the box, which, for you non-football fans, means they're bringing most of the team to cream the quarterback—me. But I've got other plans.

"Omaha!"

I stand up straight and start pointing and waving, gesturing like the pros do on television. It makes no sense, but on the other side the helmets are swiveling so I keep making up words.

"Buttermilk biscuits, orange juice..."

I glance over my shoulder. Luke is looking at me like I've spilled my brain, which is kind of the point. The defense is all sorts of confused. Just before a delay of game penalty, as I'm running out of random stuff to call out, the ball finds my hands. I fake a handoff left. The defense bites and I dash right. A large, rabid linebacker breaks loose from the pack and barrels towards me. *This is it,* I'm thinking, *he's going to knock my helmet into the stands.* But at the last second I fake left and he tackles air.

The crowd comes alive. I shake a defender and he loses a cleat. Another defender comes but I jet past him, then I shake a third one before scooting twenty-five yards where I safely duck out of bounds. Jogging back to the huddle, Coach Jackson slaps my helmet. "Way to think on your feet, Colton. But run the plays I call, got it?"

I shoot him a look like, *Did you just see what I did?* But he simply nods and points to the field. A few slaps on the back. In the huddle, the guys are howling.

"Buttermilk biscuits?" Luke asks.

I toss up my hands. "Hey, it worked didn't it?"

On the next play Luke shuffles ahead for two yards up the middle. Coach's call. Then three more on a sweep right. Again, Coach Jackson. Third and five and Coach sends in another run and I sigh. I can't believe it. He doesn't trust me to pass, even after how I've been airing it out in practice. I mean, hello, I disintegrated a tackle dummy.

It's time to show him the light.

The guys are feeling it. Hillsdale's not so big and bad. We can do this. And the linemen are enjoying my random calls, even offering up different foods to call out at scrimmage.

I turn to Harrison. "How about that post route?"

His face goes so bright it dims the evening sun. "Word."

"On three, ready, break."

At the line of scrimmage, Hillsdale crams the line, again ready to bring the house. So again I crank up the crazy talk. "Yellow light. Dog bones. Ready, Snickers bars, hut hut, hut!"

They come in heaps. Linebackers first, some untouched because Luke isn't the best at picking up a blitz. But I've learned a thing or two from my time on the bench, so I've pretty much banked on that. I duck the first one then step up, shuffling my feet as I wait for Harrison to shake the cornerback. Just as I'm running out of time he hits the jets and breaks free. I plant my magical feet and sling the ball, getting clobbered as I let it go.

Trapped under the dark abyss of Hillsdale stink, I hear muffled cheers. Our cheers? I fight and claw my way out of the pile of arms and legs and bodies to the light where I get to my feet. Down the field, Harrison is in the end zone, getting mobbed by blue jerseys.

We scored.

I say it out loud. "Hey, we scored!"

I brush myself off and rub my hands together. "Well guys, it's been fun!" I say to the goon squad, skipping for the end zone to join the celebration.

I don't make it.

"Colt! Over here!"

Coach Jackson is halfway out on the field and looking very much like a former linebacker. The kicking unit trots out, smacking my helmet in passing. Everyone is cheering. I motion towards the end zone, trying to tell our coach that we've scored, because maybe he doesn't know. But he jerks me by the facemask. "Just what are you doing?"

Um, scoring touchdowns?

I steal a glance at the end zone. The ref tosses a flag for delay of game, moving us back, and we're already in trouble when it comes to kicking because Trayvon usually handles that too. But the crowd (we have a crowd!) is going nuts.

"Um, Coach. We scored."

What I want to say is, *We freaking scored on Hillsdale, thanks to me.* But he's so steaming mad I keep things brief.

"I don't care. When I call a play, you run that play. This isn't the NFL! You don't go out there and call an audible. You could've gotten killed with that nonsense!"

Okay, apparently Coach Jackson has some major control

issues. I nod, trying to speed things along so I can join in the celebration. You know, because again, WE SCORED. Coach finally releases me just as Luke tries to kick the extra point and the ball hits our own center in the back. Who cares? I skip over to the bench for some back slapping and high-fives, a defiant smile pressed onto my face. Coach should be thrilled. I'd just tossed a perfect touchdown pass. So what I changed his stupid play?

Unlike Coach Jackson, Zach is hysterical. "Dude, that was AMAZING!" He's standing on the bench, trying to see over the linemen. I lift my helmet from my head and let out a sigh.

Zach's smile falls. He looks around. "Um, what's wrong with you?" He leans closer, nodding at my shoes. "Need more glitter?"

"Nope," I say, wiping at my tights. Around my ankles is a pinkish glow. I tuck it in my sock. "Seems Coach Jackson doesn't appreciate thinking on your feet."

I can't hear much of what he says after that because McKenzie is smiling at me from the track. Then the rest of the offense storms over and swarms me.

Harrison leads the way. I think it's his first touchdown all year because Trayvon always runs the ball in. "My man! Nice throw!"

"I wish I could have seen it!"

Luke plops down, getting an extra dose of ribbing for his flubbed kick. But we're all smiles, and it's a little bit weird having the guys over at my end of the bench. I lose Zach in the shuffle as an endless wave of high fives come my way. Coach Barber—a guy who appreciates a little improv—looks ready to split his pants he's so excited. But King Buzzkill is sulking on the sidelines, arms crossed and scowling, giving me the side eye.

Hillsdale scores before we can finish celebrating. Fine with me, I'm all about showing Coach more of what I've got. I yank on my helmet, ready to have some fun, when he grabs me by the shoulder pads, all huffy and puffy.

"Run the plays, okay?"

I give him a stiff nod. But really, what is he going to do if I don't? Bench me? Against Hillsdale? I'd like to see him try. I take one look at the crowd, on their feet, ready for more fireworks. It's like a dream come true.

Until we run Coach's plays. On first down Luke is stood up for a loss. On second down the same play nets maybe two yards. Unbelievably, Coach Jackson calls for yet another hand off.

I know he's trying to prove a point. But so am I. I scan the crowd. The cheerleaders, the coaches. The Peakland faithful. All the cheering fills me with energy, has me lightheaded with confidence. I don't want to disappoint. So I take my huddle by the eyes. "Okay, let's change this up a bit."

The guys tighten, all smirks. Austin, one of our offensive linemen, places his order for steak biscuits. I call the play. My play.

"Steak biscuits on three."

Lining up, calling out our gibberish, I look over to the sidelines and catch Coach Jackson's eyes. They seem to be daring me to defy the call. I lick my fingers and set my feet. My very um, glittery feet.

"Hike!" I pitch the ball left, just like Coach called. But Harrison rips back around and Luke flicks it to him on the reverse. The defense shifts as they react, and when they do, I spin away and break back around, cutting towards Harrison who pitches the ball to me for a double reverse. By then I can almost hear Coach's nostrils flaring, but I have the ball in stride with nothing but open field and the back of Luke's jersey leading the way.

Luke makes the one block he needs to make, smashing the poor Hillsdale safety into the next zip code. I tear down the sidelines in a trail of smoke, taking one quick glance over to find Coach Jackson's face stretched tight as stone. He is so going to kill me. But not before one last Hillsdale defender makes a break at me from an angle. Too late. I leap over him and into the end zone.

Touchdown Peakland.

Sixty-five yards. It's a thing of beauty. Coach Barber had us run this trick play at the end of my super practice, after Coach Jackson had filled our young minds with proper technique and boring drills. We named it the Loopity Loop.

Again, the crowd goes bonkers. Hillsdale looks like they don't know what hit them. I stand up only to get mobbed in the end zone, which is good because I already know Coach is waiting for me.

Flags rain down on the field for excessive celebration. I emerge from the wreckage of bodies ready to go take my licking. Unbelievably, Coach Jackson is calm and collective. Just one extra-long look and then a nod. I brush past him for the bench.

More high-fives, more cheering. This time Luke kicks a knuckle ball through the upright. After a short kickoff, Hillsdale starts the next drive at the forty-eight yard line, but who cares if they score? We can do this all night long.

At least that's what I'm thinking.

Chapter 14
Benched

After Hillsdale plugs it in for another touchdown, I wiggle my head into my helmet and set one sparkly cleat on the field. It's like the glitter has spread, working its way up my calf. But a giant hand stops me cold. "You're done, Colt."

Bad time for a joke, I'm thinking. But Coach Jackson looks serious. The guy is actually benching me. I stand there, astounded as Luke shuffles out to the field to play quarterback, looking back again to make sure this is really what we're doing.

Confusion hits the stands, a smattering of groans. Some of the Peakland JV guys—older brothers and cousins—have popped up in the crowd, and I want to show off some more. And the rowdier parents aren't shy about letting Coach know their true feelings.

All I can do is shake my head. Here I'm having a career night, and he's pulling this crap? Against Hillsdale, too.

No surprise the offense sputters. A quick three and out (maybe because our running back is playing quarterback and kicker), and we punt the ball away to a chorus of jeers and gripes at our backs. At one point I even turn around and shrug. If Coach cares, he doesn't show it.

We quickly fall behind 28-13. The team deflates. Coach Barber is in Coach Jackson's ear, but Coach Jackson never even looks my way. He doesn't address the obvious. And the defense is heated too, because without me they've been camped out on the field. The crowd continues with the booing and shouting at Coach.

Zach sneaks down to the bench. "Hey, this is crazy, huh?"

"Yeah," I say, looking around. A collective groan carries through the crowd as we set up to punt yet again.

"So uh, we did the wave earlier, did you see?"

"No, I must have missed it."

"Oh, we'll do it again. Hey, check it out. I got them chanting 'Colt the Bolt'. So why did Coach bench you?"

I shrug. "He says I'm not running his plays."

"You're running everywhere else though. Oh, check it out. Sheriff Willoughby clocked you doing twenty-four miles per hour—give or take."

"What?"

"Yeah." He nods to the far end zone, where the sun falls in the distance. "He's set up in the parking lot, watching the game."

I turn and see the squad car sitting at the curb. "No way."

Trayvon limps over just as the defense staggers back out to the field. "Looking good out there, Cold Cuts. But you gotta run the plays."

I shake my head. "The plays aren't working."

Trayvon smiles like he knows something I don't. His gaze falls to my socks, covered in glitter. He gives me a smirk. Nods towards his dad. "Trust me. Run his plays first, then you can do the fun stuff, okay? I'll talk to my dad."

"Really?"

He smiles. "Yeah man, we have to get you back out there. Break this losing streak. Nice tights, by the way. And glitter."

"Oh, yeah, I'm, uh..."

Zach slaps my back. "He stepped in a science project earlier. You know Clutts, right?"

Trayvon nods. Says he'll see what he can do. But I stay parked on the bench for the rest of the half. Coach never so much as looks back my way. Not when Marty Johnston's dad yells, "Put Clutts back in, you imbecile!" Or when the whole crowd starts chanting, *Colt the Bolt...Colt the Bolt.* Nope, he just lets me sit there, like the old days, when Trayvon was the man and I was just some scrub on the team.

By halftime, the guys are moping around, slouched and shaking their heads because for a while there, we almost had a chance at history. Now we're down again, and it's looking like it's only going to get worse when Coach Jackson calls me over. Actually, both coaches call me over. One like a storm cloud, the other looking a little giddy.

Coach Jackson speaks first. "Colton, we'd like to talk to you."

I look off to the distance. I'm not exactly in the mood for apologies, in fact, if Coach Jackson isn't going to play me, I'd rather not waste my time.

"Coach, I uh, Look, if I'm not—"

Coach Jackson sets a hand on my shoulder pads, his face still stern, but his voice a bit softer. "Listen Colt, before you say something you'll regret, Coach Barber has an idea, and," he pauses and wipes his face. He looks a little baffled, like he can't believe what he's saying.

"Well, we had a little discussion. I'm going to relinquish offensive duties. Coach Barber will take over. I'll shore up the defense. Maybe everything will work out for the best."

Behind Coach, the restless crowd only stares at Zach, who's trying to orchestrate the wave. The cheerleaders cartwheel out to the field. On the other end, the Hillsdale guys are already celebrating over on the sidelines. It so could have been us. Wait. What did he just say?

I look up at Coach. "Really?"

Coach Barber chuckles, steps forward, boiling over with glee. "Yeah, kid, you bet. Now come on, we've got work to do."

Coach Barber takes me under his girth and I'm expecting some pointers. "So what's the plan?"

I break free from his clutches. His eyes are glazed as he looks me over. I hop in place, waiting for insight. Instruction. A game plan. I'm used to Coach Jackson's tactical approach, but Coach Jackson is gone, gathering up the defense to go over strategy.

Coach Barber's face burns red with excitement or panic, it's hard to say. It's just, well, red. He grabs my helmet with both hands, his eyes bulging and his ruddy cheeks flapping. I tap around some, still waiting for some sort of, well, coaching. Instead, he says the following: "Okay Clutts, this is your big chance. Now go make something happen."

"I'm sorry, what?"

"Run kid. Do what you do. I'm giving you full reign over the offense. Just don't quit the team. Is there anything else you need? Gatorade? Anything?"

Another glance at Coach Jackson, calm and even with the defense as he points to something on a clipboard. And here's Coach Barber, telling me to score. All I can do is shrug.

"Uh, no Coach. I'm okay."

Two minutes and counting until the second half begins. And the team is fired up with the news I'm going back in. I keep an eye on Coach Jackson, wondering why he gave in so quickly. It's not like him to change his mind like that. But there's no time for him, I've got a team to lead.

And I'm off to lead when I realize I might be in a little bit of trouble. As I rush out to the field for warm-ups, my knee buckles and I go for a flop, falling on my face. It's all too Clutts-like.

Phillip calls me "same old Cold Cuts." He's right, too. My feet are a couple of cinder blocks. Cold sweat on my back, chills up my spine. Because if what I think is happening is actually happening, I'm going to be in worse shape than our tackling dummy.

Chapter 15
Technical Difficulties

I hobble over to the goalpost and fumble with my shoe. Out on the field, Coach Barber is all smiles, yukking it up with Harrison. We're about to kick the ball off and there's only 48...47...46...seconds until the second half begins. I hold up the shoe and take a peek. The glitter—the beautiful, glowing glitter—is nothing more than sand.

Okay, so it seems the more energy I burn, the faster the potion wears off. I'll take it up with Abby later, but for now I've got to come up with something quick. Only, the vial is in my gym bag. And my gym bag is under the bleachers.

I get my shoe on and stumble out to Coach Barber. "Hey, uh, Coach. I need to go to the bathroom."

Coach Barber eyes the clock. "What, now? It's game time. Can't you hold it?"

I shake my head. "No, Coach, sorry."

He shoots me a nervous glance, another peek at the clock. "Well, okay, but, hurry."

The parents cheer as I approach the bleachers. A couple great plays and privacy is a thing of the past. I nod and smile, stumble, and then find my bag in a pile of LL Beans and JanSports. I snatch it by the drawstrings and dart for the bathrooms, only I trip over my feet again and nearly impale myself on a fence post in front of the student section. I'm fading fast, and regular old Cold Cuts will soon be making a mess of things if I don't hurry.

I bust in the bathroom and slam the door, sealing off the crowd noise.

"*Colt the Bolt! Colt the Bolt!*"

Great. Zach has started a trend.

A whistle on the field signals kickoff. Time to get to work. I slip off a cleat and dab a generous shake into the heel. *Twenty-four miles-per-hour, huh,* I'm thinking, giving the vial an extra shake. *Let's see if we can clock twenty-six.*

When that glittery sparkle comes to life it's like scoring another touchdown. I dab the other shoe and cap the vial and start to put it back in the bag, but then I stop. At this pace I might need it again. Besides, Abby can always make more. I toss another dash into my palm and rub my hands together. Might as well go big.

I lace up and take the field like a comet, bolt to the sideline where Coach Barber pulls me in. "Whoa Clutts! You okay? Oh man, please tell me you're okay?"

"Much better, Coach, thanks." It's like wrestling a grizzly bear the way he has a hold of me out on the sidelines. A bit embarrassing. Finally, he realizes how awkward this must look and sets me free. He waves Luke in.

"Okay, Colt. Go out there and win!"

I search his face, waiting for the punchline. But the guy is stone cold serious. *Wow, that's some deep stuff, Coach.* Just think how many coaches could save their jobs, if only they would implement the *Just Win* strategy.

By the time I take the huddle it's third and fifteen. Luke is covered in grass stains and eager to give up the quarterback position. I take a look around. Coach Jackson stares out to the field like it's an ocean.

I can hear him now, stressing balance on offense, making adjustments and plugging in new assignments. How to play the right way. He'd have us...*whoa*... I catch myself. What am I thinking? I'm free from Coach Jackson's fundamentals. Besides, my feet are tap dancing again. I'm all set for take-off.

And now there's no one holding me back.

I flap my arms and roll my neck. The crowd erupts into cheers. Even our huddle is clapping as I take the helm. Coach Barber has given me specific instructions: Score.

"Okay guys, let's go to work."

Having already taken what they thought was our best shot in the first half, the Hillsdale guys are chatty. They take the line looking ready to pounce. But I can really feel the magic in my cleats at the snap count, tickling my toes and fingers, shooting down my arms and legs. I think it feeds off adrenaline. And I've got plenty of that at the moment. I'm supercharged, holding myself back, harnessing the energy so I won't just blast off into the sky.

Faking the hand-off, I roll right. The defense barrels down on me. Luke falls into a gap behind a group of slobbering linebackers, waving for the ball. But like I said about the energy, my feet are happy—too happy.

I fake the screen pass to Luke and take off. *Zoom.* It's like I'm running down a mountain, flying ten yards down the field before the first defender makes an appearance. Luke, probably tired from all the extra work, misses the block. No problem, I leap over the defender lunging for my legs, placing one magical cleat on his helmet and using it to spring into the air.

The crowd gasps, and I smile so big my mouthpiece goes flying. My feet hit the ground in stride. I spin off the safety and put a juke on the cornerback. He tackles air, joining the other would-be tacklers as I zip into the end zone at a warp speed pace.

Touchdown.

Third and fifteen? Ha. No problem.

Coach Barber flat out tackles me. Thunders onto the field

and blindsides me. I'm smothered by three offensive linemen on top of that, and it feels like an elevator has landed on my back. More flags as they yank me off the ground, hoist me up, and I guess someone tells them it's only the third quarter because Coach gets himself together and holds up two fingers, meaning go for the two-point conversion.

Easy. I snap the ball and leap over the line. Just like that, it's 28-21. I trot over to the sidelines, strutting past a stoic Coach Jackson, off to greet my adoring fans.

By the time I take my place on the bench, working out a few plays with Harrison, Coach Barber screams, motioning for us like a third base coach as he squeals, "Fumble! Fumble! Offense!"

I grab my helmet.

The rest of it is a blur. I take the field and hold nothing back. On first down, I run seventy yards for a touchdown. *Seventy yards* without getting touched. The crowd finally does that wave. And let the good times roll. Sherriff Willoughby has the lights going on his squad car. It's an all-out party at Peakland Middle School.

We miss the extra point and on the following possession Hillsdale finds the end zone. We've got ourselves a game. I go in and break off a forty-yard run. Then I toss a twenty-yard touchdown pass to Harrison. We go for two again, where I rush to the left, spin off a lowly defender and scamper back the other direction, high-stepping my way into the end zone. Tie game, 35-35

Back and forth it goes. By the fourth quarter, Zach is working the crowd and has officially become my public relations manager. A middle school football game quickly becomes legendary. The hashtag, #ColttheBolt hits top trending. Even the WPRK news crew arrives on the scene, the truck parked behind one end zone where there's a wall of bodies in the stands. I just hope Coach Jackson realizes what he almost lost with his stubbornness.

With just under two minutes left in the game, we get the football back, down 49-43. Coach Barber turns to me with the play. "Go score a touchdown."

The guy is a regular Bill Belichick. In the huddle, I look the guys over. "Ready. Let's do it."

My stats are off the charts. I haven't thrown an incomplete pass all night, and I want to keep things perfect. At some point, I even dipped into my vial and put a few flakes on my hands.

On first down I hit the line of scrimmage with a smirk and crank up the gibberish. "Hammocks, cheddar melts, shrimp scampi, hike, hike!"

The blitz comes storming and there is nowhere to go. Correction. There is nowhere for a mere mortal to go. My feet, however, have other plans.

They take me left. And when I say *they*, I really mean it. My feet are driving and I'm only hanging on for the ride. A wall of defenders close but I find a crack of daylight in the middle. I slip between two hefties but more come calling. At the last second, I catch a glimpse of Harrison streaking down the sidelines with a couple steps on his guy.

I chuck it with everything I've got.

The pass flutters in the wind. Harrison slows, his facemask to the sky as he makes the adjustment. A roaming defensive back converges on what should be an easy interception. What happens next will be discussed for years.

Doing all that running, I hadn't put enough muscle into the pass, so the ball floats like a sagging balloon at a parade. The safety arrives perfectly on time to make the play, but it's like someone has hit the pause button. The balloon slows to a magical stop in midair. I mean, the football halts and hangs there, like a cloud, until the poor safety goes crashing into his own bench.

Only then does the football drop safely into Harrison's hands, where he stands stock still, looking down at the ball like it's a meteor rock. Hundreds of jaws drop in complete silence. Finally, Coach Barber cries out for him to run, and he mechanically jogs into the end zone.

No one chases Harrison. Probably because no one knows what in the heck they've just seen. Me included. Without peeling his eyes away, the referee slowly finds his whistle and eventually, cautiously, raises his hands to signal a touchdown.

Both sides of the bleachers are as quiet as a library.

Chapter 16
Investigative Journalism

The seconds tick off the clock. Hillsdale fails to score, and the streak comes to an end. Our end zone is a complete circus. Cheering and whooping and I'm going to need a new jersey because mine is ripped off my back in the mayhem after the game. But whatever, we've done it. Harrison shakes up a soda and douses everyone like we've won the Super Bowl.

Coach Barber wipes his face, and it's hard to tell if its Sprite or tears streaming down his chubby cheeks. "Great game, fellas. Just great. Hey, Colt the Bolt, get over here."

I try, and fail, to imagine any situation where Coach Jackson would call me "Colt the Bolt." It's pure chaos. And in the midst of it—as I'm grabbed, shaken, shoved, and nookied so many times on my way through the bodies that I worry something in my brain might jostle loose—no one seems to notice or care that I have glitter all over my shoes, socks, my tights, and my hands.

Coach pulls me in his grasp. Yep, tears.

For the first time in my life I'm the hero, not the chump. I haven't slipped or tripped or flopped (besides that halftime trip to the bleachers). I've been cool and calm under pressure. It's crazy. Only the ginger ale in my hair reminds me I'm not dreaming. This is real.

"I think we can all agree that Clutts here deserves the game ball," Coach Barber says, thrusting the football into my gut. "Way to play, kid. I knew you had it in you. Even that last pass."

A few smiles drop at the mention of that pass, but Coach

Barber only shrugs. "Hey, I don't know what that was, but it worked."

He's right about that. The way the ball hung in the air. While physics geeks might be baffled, I know exactly how it happened. It's all over my hands. But the way I see it, this is my time. I'm due. I don't owe an explanation to anyone. Certainly not the school reporter, Jada Johnson, who's armed with a notepad and phone, waiting to speak to me.

With her tightly yanked ponytail and piercing eyes, Jada is capable of manufacturing a buzz around school quicker than an approaching snowstorm. An eighth grader, she's covered it all, from last year's stink bomb incident to the cafeteria nutrition fiasco. She's a pro. And so I know the questions are coming.

As we break from the huddle, Coach Barber announces the pizza's on him tonight, and we scatter our separate ways. I try, unsuccessfully, to slither out amongst the bodies, but parents and kids and everyone else wants a high-five from the new superstar quarterback.

But Jada is too good to be outmaneuvered. Despite my efforts, she's poised and ready, her scarf knotted around her neck and her phone aimed my way. "Colt, great game out there tonight. Congratulations on snapping the losing streak against Hillsdale. Can you tell me about that last play?"

That's Jada, right to the point. Thankfully, Zach is prepared. He slings an arm around me for support as I scrape up some words and try to arrange them into something acceptable.

"Uh, that was all Harrison, he just made a play on the ball," I say, deflecting blame, credit, weirdness. Whatever happened. I've heard the pro players say stuff like that and I like how it sounds. Besides, it definitely sounds better than "fairy dust."

Jada keeps digging. "Yes well, some fans close to the field are reporting something about a trick ball or levitation. Any truth to those claims?"

A chill wiggles up my spine. "I, uh..."

Zach scoffs. "Levitation. Really Jada? *Really?*" He sets his free arm between us like he's making way through real paparazzi. It saves me from saying something stupid. "Oh, and I think there was a phantom playing linebacker. And don't forget the trolls. Dracula kicking field goals. I mean, come on. You're better than this, Jada."

In a momentary lapse of professionalism, Jada wrinkles her nose at Zach. Then she turns back to me, tightening her grip on the phone. "So, is there any truth to the rumor about a possible quarterback controversy brewing on the Panthers' team?"

Controversy? I turn to Zach who's already shaking his head. "No comment."

I'm thinking sports agenting might be in his future. His answer earns him a sharp glare from the reporter. Jada moves on. "Colton, can you tell us why you were benched in the first half? My sources tell me you repeatedly ignored play calls. Also, is it true Coach Jackson relinquished his offensive coaching position? And if so, why the sudden shake up?"

I blink with each follow up. How does she get her info so fast? And a three-part question at that. Lucky for me, Zach brushes her off. "We have no...further...comment," my agent repeats, whisking me out towards the bleachers. Over my shoulder, I watch Jada approach Coach Jackson and Trayvon.

Zach pulls me together. "Okay man, I think she has a mole on the team. Your job is to find out who's feeding her info. If she finds out about the fairy dust, well..."

Before he can say anything else, Coach Barber plods over and shakes me one more time. His face is red and his eyes wobbly. I'm not sure what the guy's got going on in his personal life, but he's about to blow a gasket. "Oh man do I have plans for this offense," he gushes. "With you out there, running around like Fran Tarkington, we're going to score a half a hundred next game."

I look at Zach, because I'm pretty sure he's just making up names. I do my best to nod him along. He gives my head two heavy pats. "Okay, I'll see you at Michelangelo's."

He storms off, whistling a happy tune. Mom and Dad cross the track and approach me cautiously. They're not overly excited, or thrilled, or all that happy even. Maybe they're just stunned I've done something right for once.

Chapter 17
Supernatural Occurrences

Abby stomps into the kitchen the next morning. Considering she weighs maybe seventy pounds, it's more like a heavy patter. But she's ticked, I can tell by her huffy sighs and the way she has her hands on her hips like Mom does whenever I bring home my report card.

I lower my phone, someone has posted the miracle football play online, but it's kind of shaky and grainy and so you don't really see the ball hang in the air. I'm a bit relieved.

She's wearing pastels today with a bow in her hair. If she doesn't want to be a witch anymore it's fine with me, I'm a step ahead of her this time.

"You okay, Abby?"

She glares at me. "I didn't help you out so that you could be a jerk."

"I'm not sure what you mean."

"Oh, you know what I mean. Showing off like that? That last pass? How obvious was that?"

I hold up my phone. "Not so much, really."

Abby flings her hair back. I return to my phone. She starts banging around dishes in the kitchen. "Well, enjoy it, because I'm through. In fact, I'm going to destroy the book."

Yawn. It was Zach's idea to cut out the middleman, or, in this case, middle-witch. Last night, I snuck into her room and stole her little black book, copied the spell, and returned it. Genius, really. Now I can start manufacturing my own glitter.

"Do what you have to do." I sigh, getting back to my twitter feed. Two thousand followers overnight. That's like, a tenth of the town, more or less. I have to admit, it feels good to have finally outsmarted my little sister.

She spins around to face me, crossing her arms. "You were showboating. Someone in the crowd said that you were calling all sorts of weird plays. And I heard you've been skipping play practice."

"Look, *Mom*. I've worked it all out. Everything is fine."

"Yeah? Did you happen to read the *Panther Press* this morning, Mr. Everything-Is-Fine?"

Gulp. "Uh, no."

"Might want to get on that."

I pull it up online. Sure enough, Jada's been busy. Even the title, *Panthers Pull Out Magical Win Against Hillsdale*, sends a chill down my back.

Jada goes on about that last pass. How the ball "levitated" and that further investigation is needed to explain the "oddly supernatural occurrences" down at Peakland Field last night.

"She sounds crazy," Zach assures me on the way to school, scrolling through his phone. "And besides, nobody reads this rag anyway. 'Oddly supernatural occurrences.' What does that even mean?" He holds up his phone. "Look, Jada's finally gone too far, she'll be laughed out of the school for this. What we need to do is capitalize on your reputation."

"Reputation?"

"Yeah, everybody's talking about the game. How you refused to call the coach's plays and did your own thing, standing up to Coach Jackson the way you did."

"That's not what I did." *Was it?*

"Well, either way. People are talking. Colt the Bolt is a dangerous man." Then, leaning in, as though spies lurk in the trees, "And we've got the recipe!"

"Yeah, but Abby..." Saying her name makes me miss how she used to look out for me, her card tricks and silly spells. I instinctively check my back pocket, almost hoping to find the four jacks. Nothing.

Zach looks up from his phone. "Abby what?"

"Nothing. Forget it."

"Look," Zach fixes his collar, head bobbing with confidence, "you do you. I'll take care of the rest, got it?"

"Yeah, okay."

"And as for Abby. Let me handle that."

I roll my eyes. For roughly two days last summer, Abby thought she had a crush on my best friend. It may have been the sun, we'd been at the pool that day, and she quickly recovered and came to her senses. But I never should have told the guy.

He gives me his best stupid smile. "I'll talk to her. She'll come around. This glitter is going to do wonders for our social life."

"Not if you keep saying things like 'social life'."

But things are happening. I walk into school and all heads turn my way. I'm an instant celebrity. I'm whisked to the production room for morning announcements, where I'm interviewed by our morning duo, Carla and Chris.

Is it true you've been contacted by Coach Hudson at Peakland High?

What about going pro? Have you given some thought about the NFL draft?

Can you talk about that trick play?

Have you read the Panther Press today?

I can't help enjoying the new attention, until Jada walks through the doors eyeing me like a bounty hunter eyes a target. But otherwise it's cool not to be the butt of a joke for once.

Between every class it's the same thing. Someone shouts, "Colt the Bolt!" and that's all it takes. The chanting begins. At lunch, I'm tempted to go over and say something to Lani, but I'd have to risk having the whole cafeteria breaking into a chant.

And things keep getting weirder. Mr. Abbott, the track coach, corners me outside the gym.

"Clutts," he says, pacing because the guy never sits still. His t-shirt hangs off his bony frame. His extra-short running shorts are only a hair shy of being inappropriate. He pauses, sets two fingers to his neck, checking his pulse. I'm about to ask if he's okay when he blurts out. "We need you. The school needs you. Tell me you'll run the mile relay."

"Oh, well, I uh...I mean,"

"Please Colt. Please. They're thinking about cutting the team altogether, but if you come out, people will care. People will see that track and field is a real sport."

I'm half expecting him to take my hands and start bawling. All I need is for Jada to come see me making some deal with the track coach. "Okay, okay, sure. I'll do it," I say, just to get him off my back.

And on it goes. *We've* beaten Hillsdale, now there's hope for Peakland High to follow suit. I'm hoping to see Lani in the hallways so I can explain about rehearsals, it's hard to see anything with people crowding my every move. By gym class, I'm too tired to do my usual dunks, and besides, I'm still worried about the glitter and what will happen if I can't pull off her recipe. I need to conserve what I can.

Crossing the parking lot to play rehearsal, my feet drag as I think about what I'm going to say to Lani, to Worsham and the cast members. I get there early, hoping to catch her alone. I duck behind cars so I'm not seen.

Walking into the auditorium, I realize it's been nearly a week since I've been to play rehearsal. I hardly have time to gather my thoughts when Mr. Worsham appears behind my back. "Mr. Clutts, is that you?"

I laugh, waving him off. But it's clear once the whole stage turns to see me, they aren't too happy. Funny, I've managed to get the whole school to love me, and these drama geeks are offended.

Mr. Worsham announces my arrival to the cast. "Well if it isn't our long lost fairy."

Lani hardly looks up from whatever she and Preston are working on. Probably making wedding plans or something. It hurts, it really does. I want to rush up onstage and apologize. But come on, I'm sort of big time right now. We beat the almighty Hillsdale. So what I had to skip a few rehearsals? I have, like, three lines.

Mr. Worsham calls things to order. Lani and Preston are prepping for a scene and our director hands me a broom and asks me to sweep up the spillage from yesterday's snowfall. It's clear what's going on, I'm going to have to earn my way back into the play.

I suppose Dad would be proud of me for sticking with it, taking the broom and dustpan with the intentions of cleaning every bit of snow from the stage. But my dad has never had a whole football stadium cheering him on, or run through a banner with his name in curly cursive, encircled with hearts. It's kind of hard to put some push in a broom after that. So I don't. When I get backstage, and Lani and Preston's scene gets under way, I duck out the side.

I'm out.

Before football practice, I hit my favorite bathroom stall, where I dab some glitter in my shoes and watch them levitate. It never gets old. I lace them up and head for the field but instead run into Coach Barber. He's sweating like he's run a marathon and all sorts of worked up. He's got about ten new schemes he wants to utilize, he shows me, thumbing through a dog-eared notebook full of double reverses and trick plays, some scratched out and scribbled and the others with so many lines and dashes and arrows it's hard to follow what's going on.

When I ask why he wants to run a fake punt on first down, he shakes his head like I'm crazy. "Because they'll never see it coming, Bolt."

He's a lunatic. But whatever, fine, I'll just call what I want anyway. I rush out to the field for practice and stop cold. Because I was expecting a regular practice on a regular day. It's sunny and clear and a little on the warm side and sure we won a big game, but here I was thinking we'd go through the motions of learning X's and O's.

Instead, the bleachers are crammed full with adoring fans. As soon as I hit the field, the music blasts from the corner of the other end zone. A hot dog vendor works the track, the steam from his cart catching in the wind. I spot a few banners with my name on them. Zach, sporting a new pair of shades, sees me and raises a megaphone.

"There he is, folks. The one and only, Colt the Bolt!"

I shrug off my confusion. I smile, wave, and then storm midfield, playing it up, shooting finger guns in the air. We've got Reston Middle coming up and it should be an easy win. It's not until I glance left, just as I'm really getting into it, that I see Abby in the bleachers. And sitting beside her is the one and only Jada Johnson.

Great. Just great.

Chapter 18
Jolly Abby

Apparently, not just anyone can boom, zap, bop, and abracadabra a magic glitter spell. After practice, Zach hauls over an industrial-sized bucket of glitter and we spend three hours trying to get the glitter to glow.

Not happening.

Zach holds my wand in one hand and my wings in the other, poring over the pages we'd copied. "Okay, read it again."

I shake my head. Stretch my arms toward the ceiling. My shoulders are sore from all the slaps and tugs around town, and I've even signed two autographs. It's getting ridiculous. Now we sit in my room with Mom's candles burning, and it smells like cotton candy. "I remember something about the moon. That's why it's not working."

Zach drops the wand. "The moon. You never said anything about *the moon*."

"Well, I remember it now. Maybe we just need to wait."

"Wait? You have like half a vial left."

"I'll stop using it at practice."

"Pff. Yeah, good luck with that."

"What's that supposed to mean?"

Zach shrugs, tosses the wings to the floor, then face-plants himself on my bed. Max bumps his head into the door, takes one look at us and all the glitter and backs off.

Trying to cast a glitter spell is harder than it looks.

Mom calls us down for dinner, and soon our spirits are

lifted by the smell of the Lasagna, my favorite. We clean up and decide to regroup later. At the table, Mom sits down across from us, beaming, her eyes all twinkles and stars. "You okay, Mom?"

Good news in our family is usually reserved for Abby—who's out with Jada—probably spilling the details of our glittery secret. Funny how just a few weeks ago my sister was looking out for big bro but now she's all about Jada.

But Mom and Dad don't even seem to notice she's missing. I guess after so many years of crushing tests and getting straight A's and even skipping a grade, I'm long overdue for the spotlight. But there's something to Mom's voice. The same thing as the game. She and Dad are happy for me sure, but it comes with a look. Slight disbelief.

Dad comes in with the gushing. "How's the superstar quarterback?"

I nod, all shucks and all. "Good, Dad. Good."

"Wow, Colt, I just, really. When did you get so fast? You were flying out there."

"I don't know, really. Just don't want to get tackled, I guess."

Zach is in a zone at the table, unflustered by our failed attempt to recreate the spell, buried in his phone and working the Twitter feed. He seems unfazed by it all. Then again, it's not exactly his life we're talking about.

The spell. Hitting the football field without the magic means certain death for me, and not only that, Jada seems to be getting closer to discovering our secret, something once thought impossible. She's relentless, hounding me in the hallways and asking me for an exclusive interview. And now she's besties with my little sister. Not cool.

Speaking of relentless, Zach has ordered two hundred *Colt the Bolt* t-shirts online, says it's never too early to start thinking about my image. It's too much.

Dad scoops out a square of lasagna, but it falls flat on the table. "Whoopsie."

Mom takes the spatula and fixes things up for him. "And now Abby is working on the school paper. It's great."

"What?" Zach and I both say in unison.

Mom smiles at Dad. "Oh yes. She's a gifted writer, you know. And she's taken a sudden interest in social issues, school funding. Even sports, Colton."

Zach sets his phone down. "Shocker."

Dad tries to get a bite on his fork but it falls to his plate. "We think it's great. I mean, I was getting a little worried with all the witchiness, but it seems the phase has passed."

"Speaking of witchiness. Where is the book of, um..." Zach's voice cracks. He clears his throat and I know where this is going. "I mean. So what did you guys do with all the witch stuff? Asking for a friend and all."

Mom and Dad laugh it off. But I'm not laughing. I've got a whole list of problems, starting with how Abby's been recruited. She's young and vulnerable and star struck by Jada Johnson, who is only using her to get to me. My only hope now is that if Abby spills my secrets, won't she sound like a lunatic? Even to Jada?

And the glitter situation. Yikes. Even if I sit out practices, it's a stretch. We still have six games left on the schedule. And track. And basketball. How am I supposed to live up to expectations? To my brand, as Zach would say. Wow, I'd almost rather just flop across the stage than deal with all of this.

Stage, *ugh*. Thoughts of theater only make me think of Lani. How I've left the cast and crew in a tough spot just a week before our big production.

Too many thoughts. I've triggered Mom's radar. "You okay, sweetie?"

"Huh? Yeah." I tear into my lasagna, chug my milk. Mom

and Dad start gushing about Abby even as this dinner was supposed to be about me and all my success. Typical.

"Isn't it great though, for her to get out and try new things?"

"Yeah, awesome," I mumble through a mouthful.

After dinner we give the glitter one more shot, but it's no use. Our only hope is to stakeout Abby's return. We flop on the couch and Zach scrolls through the feed, humming the theme from Sonic the Hedgehog until the lights hit the driveway.

Max goes crazy. From the window, we watch as she gathers her book bags—because Abby has two—and says goodbye. Soon as she walks through the door, Zach and I pounce.

"Abby. We need to talk."

She looks at me, then Zach. "Guys, I'm really busy."

I scoff. "Oh, let me guess, you and Jada Johnson are hot on a story, is that it? A story that involves a certain quarterback on a certain football team, huh?"

Abby shifts one bag on her shoulder, they seem to be weighing her down. She looks exhausted as she starts towards the kitchen, waving me off like she doesn't have time for me. "If you must know, we were covering the Peakland JV game against Hillsdale. It wasn't pretty."

"I can't believe you won't help me, Abby," I sigh. "Your own brother."

Max jumps as she lets the bags drop to the floor. Zach looks up from his phone. Sure enough, Max tucks his tail and scampers out of the room, probably thinking a thunderstorm is rolling in, off to look for a bed to hide under. Abby shakes her head. "Colt, come on. I *am* helping you."

"Right. Helping me. By hanging with your new friend. Let me ask you this, Abby. Did it ever dawn on you that maybe, just maybe, Jada Johnson is only buddying up with you, letting you write for the paper, to get to me? Have you thought of that yet?"

Soon as it leaves my mouth I want it back. My words hit her

hard, and when they do I see my little sister again. Not this new Abby, but the old one. The one who always looked up to me. She looks crushed.

She wipes back her hair, takes a big breath, and sighs. "Gee, silly me. And all this time I thought it was because I was a good writer. You really know how to make someone feel great about themselves."

"Abby, look. I'm sorry, it's just that I'm running out of glitter and—"

"You know, last winter, when I first started my spells and potions, I knew Mom and Dad thought it was weird. And sure, you made fun of me, but we were at dinner one night and I'll never forget something you said. You said what you loved most about me was that I knew how to be myself. Do you remember that?"

I do remember. Abby has always done her own thing and not cared what people thought. "Abby, I'm sorry."

She shakes her head, waving me off. "I think it's time you took your own advice."

Chapter 19
Big Time

F riday is a mess. Abby won't speak to me and Zach won't stop with his publicity campaign. He's calling it a campaign, by the way. On the way to school he tells me his plans to rent a billboard and how he thinks we should look into a cannon for the northeast end zone. The only thing that gets him to stop talking is when we get to the parking lot and a shadow like a storm cloud passes over us. "Hey, you Clutts?"

We both look up, way up, to find Porkchop Peterson, the hulking right guard on the Peakland varsity football team. Zach takes a step back. "Whoa."

I nod, slowly, wondering why this giant is visiting our middle school. Sometimes the varsity guys will stop by for pep talks or mentoring, but Porkchop looks like he's got something on his mind. He also looks out of breath from the walk across the lot.

He nods at me. "Coach wants to see you."

"Coach?"

"Yeah. Coach Hudson."

"Oh, um..."

A mile of a smile spreads across Zach's face. "Wait, he wants Colton? He does, doesn't he?" He nudges me in the ribs. "This is it. This is your time to shine."

Porkchop shrugs. "He just told me to get The Bolt." He looks down to me again. "You The Bolt? You seem kind of shrimpy."

Zach sets a hand on my shoulder. "Yes, this is him. Let's go."

Porkchop shakes his head. "Nope, just him. Sorry dude."

Zach cheers as I'm escorted across the lot to the high school. I have a pass of some sorts, a note from Coach Hudson himself. The guy has been the coach of Peakland High since my dad was a kid. He's won five state championships, but lately things have dried up, roughly around the same time Hillsdale built their powerhouse. The town hangs on to Hudson mostly out of tradition, but even I know that a few more losses to Hillsdale and well, traditions change.

I enter Peakland High, with its endless hallways and faint musty smells. Again, I've only set foot in the theater and the gymnasium to catch a basketball game. Now I'm walking past the lockers, in the midst of laughter and mayhem, going to see Coach Hudson. Crazy.

Porkchop shoves some kids in passing, laughing and calling out to other meaty linemen and football players in shiny jerseys. He shakes his head, nods to someone in passing. "The JV guys got smoked last night."

He drops me off in an office where the legend himself awaits. Trophies and plaques line the walls. Old Hudson's got a helmet full of hair, shiny and silver. His ruddy cheeks worn from wind and cold from all those deep playoff runs into winter.

"Colton," he says from behind a desk. He motions for me to shut the door. I do, then stand there as he sizes me up. The bell rings out in the hall. Coach Hudson gestures to the chair in front of his desk. "Have a seat."

With the door shut and my butt in a chair, the old coach sits back, his hands clasped behind his head. "You know, there's a saying we have at Peakland. We're all family here. From kindergarten to graduation."

I nod, wondering if this is really happening. Is he asking me to play varsity?

"I've been watching you play, Colton, running up and down the field, slinging the ball around, playing to the crowd. It's quite something, really."

"Thanks, Coach," I say, still wondering where this is going. What I'm doing here. I think back to what Zach said, about this being my time to shine. But dude, I'm twelve.

He leans forward, sets a hand to his chin, a state championship ring about the size of a golf ball on his finger. "What's your secret?"

My laugh doesn't sound like my own. "I uh, no secret, just practicing, I guess."

He nods, all business like. "I need you Clutts. We need you. We gotta end this losing streak to Hillsdale. I'm sure you heard about the JV guys last night, those boys got crushed. We need you to come out tonight and give us a boost."

Tonight? It jolts my attention, for the first time I look into his hazy gray eyes. "Wait, do you mean—I'm still..." I look around for cameras, because this has to be a gag. Then, with a shrug. "I'm still in middle school, Coach."

He waves me off, a mere practicality. "Right. Did you know Serena Williams won Wimbledon when she was thirteen?"

"No, um, I don't think that's right."

"Got kids going pro in basketball. You're Peakland, you're family. And your family needs you, Colton."

"Oh." I take inventory in my head. How much glitter is left compared to the truckloads of it I would need to play varsity football without being squashed like a bug on a windshield.

"I spoke to your principal. Big football guy, that one." Coach Hudson stands, adjusts his waistband, then thrusts his hand over the desk. "Welcome to the Panthers, kid. Be down on the field around five."

We shake. "Here." He reaches in a box, throws a jersey my way. I miss it and it lands on my face, not exactly displaying my athletic prowess. I pull it down. Shimmering blue. Number two.

"See you tonight, kid."

So many questions. But I think Coach Hudson—*the* Coach Hudson—has just named me the starting quarterback of the Peakland High School football team. I'm not sure about legal implications or what Mom might think about this, but Zach is going to freak out.

I dash across the parking lot, nearly getting creamed by an empty bus pulling out. I've got to be careful, and I have to use my glitter wisely.

By lunch word has spread throughout the school. Between Zach hyping the news and that I was spotted walking with Porkchop Peterson across the parking lot, it's a given something is up. And there's no ducking Jada Johnson, who seems to know everything, even my jersey number. She may as well have been in Coach Hudson's office with me.

She finds me in the hallway just after Zach leads a *Colt-the-Bolt* cheer in the cafeteria. "Colton, is it true you will be playing quarterback for Peakland High, and, if so, isn't that a blatant violation of VHSL rules?"

In her hand is an official Virginia High School League rulebook. I'm fumbling over words when Zach throws an arm around me and steers me clear. "Just won't let it go, will you, Jada."

"No," she says without laughing. "I won't."

That afternoon, Abby is nowhere to be found. She's not in the cafeteria. She's not in the newsroom (which is actually just Mr. Tim's History classroom) when I fly by, risking a Jada sighting. I need to find her and apologize. I think I have enough for the game this evening, barely. Still, we need to talk.

With my mind spinning out of control, I can think of only

one place to go to calm my pregame jitters. I enter the dark auditorium, where I sneak into a seat near the back and watch play rehearsals until it's time to get moving.

Chapter 20
The Deal

I get lost looking for the Peakland High School locker room. By the time I find it, the team is warming up on the field. And that's fine, I need a minute to myself, to savor this brief moment of calm before whatever craziness is about to come my way. I take out my jersey, run a finger along the stitching, and tell myself this is not a dream. But it's time to get moving.

I break out the vial, about to add a dash to my sneakers when I hear someone enter. A large shadow. I slide the vial back into my bag.

"Colton."

Coach Jackson, like a forgotten friend, in his street clothes. He looks more relaxed than I've ever seen him. His usual scowl is gone, replaced by what could pass for a smile. Stranger than that is how I'm kind of glad to see him. "Hey, Coach. What are you doing over here?"

"Just visiting." His gaze finds my jersey. "Well, you're certainly having yourself quite a run, huh?"

I shake my head. "It's kind of crazy."

The old wooden bench strains under his weight as he takes a seat beside me. Coach isn't fat, but solid. Trayvon brags about how he played division two ball before he blew out his knee. Must've been the left one because he seems to favor it as he leans forward.

"Look, I'll make this quick. First, I want you to know I'm proud of you. You've been playing great lately." He chuckles.

"Better than great, and I never doubted what you could do, I just wanted you to do it the right way, got it?"

The middle school game seems like a year ago. Any hard feelings between us are long gone. But sitting beside Coach—the guy who stuck with me when I was Cold Cuts the third stringer, brings on a tidal wave of shame. I haven't done anything the right way. It's all smoke and mirrors. Well, dust and glitter, but either way I'm nothing more than a phony. A really fast phony who's dug a hole too deep to climb out of now.

He pats my knee. "Well, that's all. Now get out there and show them what you got." Then, with a chuckle, he adds, "I don't know what kind of strings Coach Hudson pulled to get this done, but listen, it's all the same. Play the game, go through your reads, and make the smart play, okay?"

"Yeah." For a split second I almost come clean. Coach has that vibe about him, makes you want to believe the best in yourself, like maybe it can all work out. But the moment passes as soon as I glance at my new shiny jersey. Besides, how would the truth sound? The truth is unbelievable.

Coach gets to his feet, pops his knee out. "Okay kid, good luck."

"Thanks, Coach."

He walks out quietly, a slight limp in his step. All that's left is a dripping sound somewhere near the showers. I'd always thought of Coach Jackson as this big, mean, invincible coach, but watching him leave, he seems all too human. The door opens and I catch the roar of the stadium, then it shuts, sealing me in with my guilt.

With the team out on the field warming up, I have a second to get my head and feet together. I drag an old chair to a shower stall for some privacy and scrounge through my bag, when the door opens again then slams shut.

I jump backward Clutts style, the chair catching my knees and well, you know, really making a mess of things.

"Who's there?"

"I knew you were up to something."

I scramble to my feet. I've dropped the vial and it's rolled out to the floor. Eyes adjusting, I make out the rust streaks and stains of the ancient shower. *Clickety-clack, clickety-clack.* A silhouette nears, a figure wearing knee high boots, a large, silver belt buckle, and a head scarf dangling over one shoulder.

"I always knew you were a joke. A goofball. A klutz. I just never knew you were a cheater."

"Preston?"

He's in full costume. I'm wondering if I've missed something. Is the play tonight? No. Just this dork in his knee-high boots clicking on the locker room floor. "Looking for something?" he says, sauntering over. *Clickety-clack, clickity-clack.* I'm getting tired of all these visitors, but all is forgotten when he holds up my vial like evidence in a courtroom. "So, what are you doing with this stuff, anyway?"

Two questions run through my mind as I take a big, stuffy locker room breath of defeat. One, how does he know anything about the vial? Two, why is he dressed like an extra for Pirates of the Caribbean? Then a third question springs to life: what exactly is school policy on fairy dust and sports? That leads to question number four: is fairy dust considered a performance enhancing drug?

Better to be vague, I figure. "Why does it matter?"

He snickers. "Oh, I think it matters more than you're letting on."

Preston's too smart and too suspicious for me to pull anything over on him. Time to negotiate. "Look, it's a good luck charm."

"It's also the property of the Drama Department," he says, all smug-like.

"That again? Dude, Mr. Worsham gave it to me."

"For football?" He clicks his teeth. "Doubt it. But you know what?" He steps closer. He's got his coat collar turned up. The guy sure is full of himself. I'm about to call him out when he tucks the vial away in his coat pocket. "Maybe I'll just hang on to this."

"Look, Preston, I really need to—"

"I mean, with you out there setting records, playing high school football and everything, I honestly don't see how you have time for the play anymore. Not with all of this."

For Preston, of all people, to ruin this. To hold my hopes and dreams in his hand as the whistle blows on the field, the band blasting away and the PA announcer revving up the home crowd for kickoff, I'm ready to start begging.

I try to keep my voice from cracking, to hang on to whatever shred of dignity I've got left. "Look, what do you want from me?"

He nods to my chair. I sit.

He kicks an empty bottle of Axe across the floor, into the shower scum of gym classes past. With an actor's flourish, he presents the vial and fiddles with the cork. I start to stand but he cocks his head. I know if I make a move, whatever's left of my glitter is toast.

He gives me a smile, taps his chin with a finger. "Hmm, what do I want? What do I want? Oh, I know. Yes. How about *you* weasel your way out of the play?"

"What?" I shout. "I did that already."

"No way. I saw you earlier, sitting in the back. You just can't stay away, can you?"

He pops the cork off the vial. I squirm, on the edge of the

chair. When he tilts the vial I can't help myself. I cave. "Okay, okay, whatever you want."

Preston stops and turns his head. "I mean it. A deal's a deal, now. If you show up again, ever, I tell everyone what's going on here."

The crowd, the whistle, the band blasting into the fight song. I have to get on the field. I shake my head. "Look, I promise. Now just give me the vial."

He stands there for nearly a full minute, enjoying every second of my agony. "Wow, Colton, and here I thought you and Lani..." He shakes his head. "I really thought you would have put up more of a fight. Well, here you go."

Preston tosses the vial, I jump, making a diving catch to keep it from hitting the concrete floor and possibly spilling. With a laugh, he heads for the door. "Man, that was easy," he says, shaking his head. Then he's gone.

Yeah, I know. Not my best moment. But I can't help myself. I'm hooked, on the fans, the cheers, the Colt-the-Bolt chants in the hallways. Once you have a taste of stardom, trust me, it's hard to let go. I take a deep breath to calm myself. I try not to think about what I've just done. I take out the vial because there's no looking back. Not now. It's Bolt time.

I dump it in my shoes, shake it out on my hands, and even with the glitter at crucial levels, I toss a little down my shirt. I'm going to need it.

Everything gets going: the foot tapping, the arm tingling. I'm ready to run. Time to Colt-the-Bolt it for the field.

Chapter 21
Showtime (Again)

For a guy who's just sold his soul to Preston the Gypsy, I'm feeling pretty good as I take the field. The thump of the crowd in my chest is magical. Stepping out, it's like I'm Lamar Jackson or something, the way they cheer. It's impossible not feed off the crowd, which erupts again when I do my signature pistols in the air routine. They eat it up. Hey, maybe I'm not Lamar, but I'm Colt the Bolt, and that's not too bad.

Here's the thing, even though I know the high school guys from watching the games, they don't know me from anywhere. I haven't even had one practice with them. Now, as I join in for warm-ups, they give me a once over. But before they start laughing, Coach Hudson waves me in. I glance at the scoreboard. Only three minutes until kick off.

"How do you feel, kid?"

"Great, Coach." Which I do, the extra dosage in my cleats feels almost dangerous, because I can hardly keep them on the ground. I'm like a hovercraft, and my fingers, well, it reminds me of the football hanging in the air like a magic trick. Now, hopping in place, it's like I've got Pop Rocks in my bloodstream.

Coach sets a hand on my helmet to keep me grounded, leaning in close, his words accompanied by the smoky scent of beef jerky. "I've been coaching this team for seventeen years and I've never seen anything like this, you hear me?" He pauses, takes a look around the stadium with a gleam in his eyes. But just when I think he's about to start crying on me, he yanks my facemask. "Tonight, we end this streak, got it?"

I don't know Coach Hudson all that well. Before this morning, I'd only seen pictures of him in the papers. Again, he's well known around town and he knows it. To hear him say it, you'd think there are plans in place to rename the stadium after him and maybe erect a statue out front. But right now, tugging on my facemask, his eyes wide and pleading, the guy looks downright terrified.

I can't help but nod. "Yes, sir."

Still clutching my helmet, Coach Hudson looks over my head and to the field. I'm getting the feeling his little pep talk is as much for himself as me. "That's the spirit, Holden."

"Colton."

"Right. I know you've got what it takes, kid. Just stay quick on your feet, because once they see you take that field they're going to bring the house, okay?"

Sure Coach, whatever. *Just let me go.*

He releases me and I stalk the sidelines while the captains go out to midfield to do the coin toss thing. The temperature has dipped and I've cooled down since leaving the locker-room. But the chill only makes me want to move more. I rub my arms, and feeling the eyes on me, I turn and shoot a wave to the crowd.

Another explosion of cheers. There's no point in looking for Mom or Dad. I know they're here somewhere in that blur of faces and hands and bouncing bodies. Maybe Abby. Jada for sure. It's hard to believe it's only been a week since I ripped my pants.

"Hey, Colt the Bolt." I turn and find Shane Peters, the senior quarterback, the guy whose job I've just taken. He motions me over with a head nod. I hustle over and look straight up, way up because Shane is like six-foot-forever. He smiles.

"Look at you, all fresh faced and ready. I remember those days…"

Not to be rude, because under normal circumstances I'd be thrilled to meet the guy I've watched from the stands so many times, but I'm a little preoccupied at the moment. It seems everyone wants my attention at once. I glance back to the field where the referee signals we've won the toss and elected to kickoff. It gives me some time to throw.

Oddly enough, Shane—with his hat on backwards—doesn't seem all that put-out to be benched. He's also on the basketball team, maybe he just doesn't want to get mangled on the field and risk being out for the upcoming season.

"Look man, I just wanted to say good luck." He looks around the stadium. "This is crazy, huh?"

I find a ball. It feels warm in my hands. "Crazy doesn't cover it."

"For real. Hey look," he says, leaning closer, a quiver in his breath. "See number fifty-eight out there? Kendell Marshall, inside linebacker. Dude is a beast. Not to scare you, but he's put out like three starting quarterbacks this year already."

Gulp. "Put *out*?"

Shane cocks his brow. "Yep. Like, *out* out. But look, he's a sucker for a pump fake. Keep that in mind and you may live to see second down. Got it?"

"Um, yeah. I think so. Thanks for the tip."

"Okay, now go warm up," he says, shoving me off.

I flip the ball in my hands. My arm feels like a rubber band pulled tight. I gaze out to the field where Kendell Marshall paces, doing what looks like a Samurai Warrior ritual. Yikes. I only hope this fairy dust lasts me through the game.

IT'S TRUE. The Hillsdale guys are giants. Angry giants. I try my best not to appear intimidated, but it's a little crazy—me being on the same field as Kendell Marshall is no joke. Especially considering I'm about as tall as his belly button.

But I'm ready to fly. A few snickers about my tights make the rounds, but I'm used to that by now. I take the huddle by storm, same as our middle school team. Only these guys have neck beards and nobody is smiling.

"Okay guys, let's go out and—"

"Seriously? What is Coach thinking?"

"Dude, are you wearing a jockstrap or a diaper?"

They start cracking up and it's Cold Cuts all over again. They have their own conversation without me, arguing over my size and asking if I still use a car seat—which I don't. I should have seen this coming. Like I'm supposed to just hop in and lead them to victory? Heck, I agree. What *is* Coach thinking?

No time for that. We're under the lights and the crowd is waiting.

Finally, Porkchop Peterson speaks up. "Well, what's the play, squirt?"

"Um, I don't know."

"What do you mean you don't know?"

I shrug. "Coach didn't give me one." He was so worked up about the game, about me, that he never even gave me a play to call. I guess that makes it my call.

A whistle. Delay of game. The crowd makes some noise and it's middle school all over again. Only it isn't. I have the glitter and I'm ready to go.

We back up and I hear the jeers from the Hillsdale side. I take the huddle, looking over the receivers. "Get open. If not, meet me in the end zone."

They exchange smirks. "You hear this kid?"

At the line, Hillsdale is drooling to get after me. I try not to look them in the eye, especially number fifty-eight, but it's hard to ignore the taunts.

The play snaps into action. From the start, it's clear Kendell Marshall and those lugs have me in their game plan. They're in our backfield before I can blink. They come fast, huffing in hot pursuit as I bail, back-peddle, then spin off, setting my free hand to the turf to catch my fall. Kendell leads the charge. He's right on my heels, and I can feel his cleats stomping after me. Just when it seems like I'm out of room—like he's going to crush me, *ZIP*. It's like I hit turbo speed.

I duck one meathead, then another one. I hurdle the next one before I blast down the sidelines. My legs chug like I'm running down a steep hill with long, galloping strides that are too long for my body. I pump my arms to keep pace, racing downfield like a rocket. I reach the end zone but I can't stop myself, even as the whistle sounds and the crowd erupts. My cleats hit the track, *click click clicking* as I burn through to the tunnel almost all the way to the locker room. Out of sight from everyone, I fall to my knees and choke down a few breaths.

Whoa.

Chapter 22
The After Party

The whole town goes nuts after Peakland High defeats Hillsdale 46-31 and finally snaps the streak. I manage to set all sorts of new records in rushing and for being all-around spectacular. Zach sends in some footage and it makes SportsCenter.

I'm not sure the records will hold, being that I'm in middle school, but people are talking. I'm doused by a Mountain Dew shower in the locker room. Coach Hudson gives me the game ball—my second in a week. I'm still wondering how he plans to keep me on the team, especially with Jada Johnson prowling around, stalking the stadium with a rulebook, but hey, I might as well enjoy the ride.

We clean up and make our way to the parking lot. I catch a ride on Porkchop's shoulders. And it's while two offensive linemen, Bear and Boar, are belting out the fight song at the top of their lungs, when sure enough, I catch sight of Jada in the crowd. She gives me a not-so-friendly wave, a wave I pretend not to see. By the time Zach rushes over to join me, I'm being tossed in a Suburban and we convoy our way to Michelangelo's, where it feels like the rest of the school has squeezed into the small restaurant.

I'm still taking it all in when McKenzie Cooper slides into my booth with wide eyes and an extra curl to her smile. "So, are you like, the starting quarterback now?"

My legs are like rubber. I only passed the ball once, to

myself—a touchdown I might add—but the rest of it was all done on my legs. I finger the laces of my game ball.

"I don't know, it depends on..."

I let the thought fade. I spot Abby at a table with Mom and Dad, pouting and rolling her eyes, looking like she's about to beg them to take her home. It's getting old. She should be happy for me.

"The answer is yes. He's the man," Zach says in between chomps of free pizza. "I mean, you're looking at a guy who just rewrote the record books. They'd have to be crazy not to start you. Oh, and I'm in the process of reaching out to some NFL scouts, get the scoop on that age requirement." He shoots McKenzie a wink. "So uh, how's Julie, anyway, since she fell off that pyramid?"

McKenzie glances at him, then she reaches out and touches my hand. "I think it's really, really cool, Colton."

It's hard to think straight when you're staring into the tropical waters that are McKenzie Cooper's eyes. I'm only reminded about my main problem—you know, glitter—when Jada Johnson blows in and takes a seat beside Abby. She says something to my sister and they look over to me. I know I'm toast.

McKenzie pats my hand again as she stands. "Well, I've got to go, but I'll see you at school, hopefully."

Hopefully. Last week she didn't know I existed. Now she can't wait to see me.

Zach's nudging me, smiling, talking about Julie, when Jada leaves Abby's table and comes marching over to me. Behind her, back at the booth, Abby only stares at the table. Something's wrong.

"Hi Colt, congrats on your big game."

Zach slaps down his slice of pizza. "What do you want, Jada."

"So," she says, ignoring my friend and going old school with a pen and pad. "You've had a remarkable streak of...good luck, shall we call it?" I push my plate away. Jada fixes her glasses. "However, there are rumors as to the source of this alleged luck."

Zach groans. "Back to that again, Jada? Come on, give it a rest."

Jada takes a breath, glances over her shoulder. "Fine. I'll go off the record." She points the pen at me. "I know something is going on. I don't know what, exactly, because *some* people aren't telling what they know. But I plan on finding out."

I pop my head up. Abby hasn't ratted me out. I can't believe it, this whole time I thought she only wanted to be popular, to impress Jada, but I was wrong. It's just me who wants to impress people.

Meanwhile, Zach lets Jada have it. "Yeah, go find out, Jada. Go and *investigate*. Oh, I know. You can start with the werewolves, and vampires, and the suuuuuupernatturaaaaaal. But if I were you, I'd stick to PTO meetings."

She rolls her eyes and spins off. Zach elbows me in the ribs. "So get this, I entered you in the Mr. Panther contest."

"The what?"

"The Mr. Panther contest. It's this old contest that's been going on at Peakland High since like, forever. Like a talent show, for beefcakes."

"I know what it is. But I'm in middle school. And, um *beefcakes*?"

"Okay yeah, it's stupid. But it's exposure."

"No thanks. Jada's all the exposure I can take right now."

Later, I'm sitting up in bed, too wound up for sleep. So much is happening so fast that none of it seems real. I flop over on one side, then the other. We've just beaten Hillsdale. My life is amazing at the moment. Only something is wrong. Way wrong.

And that's when reality sacks me. What I've agreed to do. What I've done to Lani, the girl who'd asked me to take the part and I said I'd do it. She'd agreed to go out with me when I was plain old me. Before the dunks and before football stardom. And now I've quit. On the play. On her.

Football. All of those fans. The same fans who laughed at my spills and snickered at my falls. Those YouTube comments. Now they love me. Or, they love The Bolt.

I throw off the covers. Another strike of terror. Because the glitter is gone. Not only have I quit the play and sort of quit on Lani, I'm all but done on the field, too. Because when the stadium lights pop to life next week, and everyone is cheering, it will be just me. Clumsy old Cold Cuts with no hope. And all that stuff Mr. Worsham said about being true to thy self, or whatever? Well, I'm the most untrue person I know at the moment.

Chapter 23
A Deal's A Deal

It rains on Saturday and all I want to do is stay in bed and be miserable, but Mom isn't buying my stomach virus excuse. Considering I feel like worm guts for what I've done, moping around like a chump doesn't take much acting. Mom makes soup, and I hole up in the basement with my phone turned off, watching movies and staring at the walls until Abby walks in.

I leap into action. "Oh, there's my darling sister."

She stops, lowers her gaze. "What do you want?"

"What do I *want*? Sheesh, come on, sis."

She gives me a look. "Sis?"

"Hey, I was thinking. Ha. Remember when we used to play Monopoly and I'd spend all my money on Boardwalk, and you would buy up the utilities and..."

"Is this going anywhere? I've got plans, Mr. Panther."

"That was Zach's doing, not mine."

"It's so stupid, this pageantry of toxic masculinity. You know, these stupid cultural traditions only—"

"So, you've got plans? Here I am trying to spend quality time with my sis and—"

Abby whirls around to face me, her voice cracking. "Just stop it, Colton. I'm not stupid. I know you what you want. Just like Jada only wants her story. It's like everyone wants to use me for something."

Her voice cracks. I've never seen my sister like this. Sure, she used to be a little brat and throw fits, but this is different. I shake my head. "Abby, look. I'm sorry, okay."

But it's too late. She's gone.

By Monday afternoon it's all I can take. I stop by the auditorium to formally quit the play. Or get kicked out, at least, is my plan, anyway. I figure I'll go in there and be so horrible no one will want me in the play. That way I'm technically not quitting. It's for the best, I'm spread too thin as it is. A deal's a deal and all. Still, it feels terrible.

Quietly, I slip through the doors. Mr. Worsham is onstage, working with Set Design to build the wedding venue. The plywood still needs to be painted and the awning is leaning to the left, but all in all it's coming along. The rest of the cast is just sort of hanging around.

Sure enough, Lani is up there getting chummy with Preston, who's looking all the more like Captain Jack Sparrow every day. I step closer, up one dark row to the next, trying to catch what they're saying about me when, well, remember I'm out of glitter?

Crash. Bang. Boom.

Everyone stops and turns. I start to duck but it's no use. Lani turns, sees me, and I'm surprised when she waves. Suddenly my shoelaces become fascinating.

It's funny how I'm the most popular kid in school at the moment. My whole History class broke into applause during first period when they mentioned my feats on Friday night. Coaches pump their fists at me in the hallways, and my hands are sore from all the high-five smacks. Coach Hudson sent Porkchop across the lot again, pulling me from math class to personally tell me that I would be starting on Friday against Sterling.

So, I'm kind of a big deal. And all of that is great. But in that auditorium, none of it matters. It's like another planet. A planet without sports.

"Mr. Clutts, what a surprise," Mr. Worsham says. "Can I help you?"

Preston's face goes tight. He's already shaking his head. I've broken the deal, and he's going to make me pay. But you know what? I'm out of glitter and out of luck. What else can he take from me?

"Um, well..."

I definitely sound like the old me again.

"We need to get started. Places, people. Colton, if you are still looking to be in the play, how about you join us?"

The next thing I know I'm climbing onto the stage. Without tights or wings or wand because it's all in my locker. Preston shakes his head and glares at me as he and Lani take their places in the forest, where the altar will go if those shop guys ever get it built. It's the big scene, where I cast my spell to stop the wedding.

With Preston glowering over there I know what I have to do, and so I put about as much effort into my role as I would taking off my dirty socks. I mean, if I'm really not going to do this thing then why bother?

"Cut."

Mr. Worsham sets a finger off his chin. "Let's try that scene again. And Mr. Clutts, how about you join us this time."

"Sure thing, Coach."

The second time I come strutting out, waving a ruler as my wand around like a goofball. I'm being a complete jerk but can't stop myself. Mostly everyone laughs, well, except Preston, which wasn't unusual. Then again, Lani isn't laughing either. She's hardly even paying attention to me.

Mr. Worsham asks for a word after rehearsal. This is it, what I'd planned, but my heart is pounding because I'm letting him down. And I'm worked up after watching Lani stroll out of the auditorium with the rest of the drama geeks. She never even glances back or says goodbye. Ouch.

Mr. Worsham starts in about commitments and our obligations to fulfill our roles. It's typical theater spiel, until lowers his head to get my full attention. It's all I can take so I just blurt it out, "Mr. Worsham, I'm sorry, but I gotta quit the play."

He stiffens, then recovers with a nod, probably about to start with the philosophical stuff when I leap off the stage, fall, then get to my feet and rush up the aisle toward the door, calling back to him over my shoulder. "Sorry, Mr. W, I just, I..."

The door clicks shut. It takes some serious scrambling to catch up with Lani in the halls. "Hey, Lani, can I uh, talk to you for a sec?"

"Um, I guess," she says, adjusting her glasses. "Are you sure you have time for me?"

Man, the smirk on Preston's face. I wonder just what Gypsy Boy has told her. It throws me off my already wobbly game.

I put some thoughts together. "Um, yeah, I was, just—"

"*Colt the Bolt...Colt the Bolt...Colt the Bolt!*"

No, no, no, not now. Bear and Boar, the mammoth twin offensive linemen scoop me up and whisk me off. Apparently, Coach Hudson wants to see me again.

I struggle to get turned around, arms out to say I'm sorry. Lani simply waves. And once again I can only watch as Lani and Preston walk off together. And again, she doesn't turn around.

Drama.

Coach Hudson announces to the team I will be starting again. He's found that loophole in the rulebook, "Probably," he mutters. And Shane completely understands. I don't think so. While he might have been fine missing the Hilldale game, judging by the death ray glare I get from him on my way out, Shane does not *completely* understand. Trust me.

The team is riding high, though, slapping my helmet and calling me The Bolt. We breeze through practice. I guess after beating Hillsdale Coach figures we deserve a break. I'm relieved because of my glitter situation, at least until afterwards, when he sets a big hairy hand on my shoulder. "Clutts, don't think I forgot about your tardiness the other night. Give me twelve laps."

Even the new star quarterback isn't untouchable, I guess. I hit the track, plodding along, trying to sort through my thoughts and worries. But with each lap around the track, my thoughts only get foggier.

Stupid Preston. Why did I agree to his deal? Because he'd had that dust in his hands and I was terrified of losing it. But by choosing the fairy dust and stardom, I'd tossed away any chance with Lani. And not just Lani, but Abby. And myself. It's nothing more than one big, elaborate lie.

And by Friday, everyone will see the ugly truth for themselves.

Chapter 24
The Glitter Effect

Things are getting out of control. It seems the entire Peakland football team took a field trip to the arts and craft store over the weekend. Zach and I laugh as we walk past the high school. Because *everyone* is wearing glitter now, including a few teachers, smacking each other on the back and laughing about who looks more like a fairy.

Not only that, Mr. Abbott is still stalking me in the halls. I'm still ducking Jada, who's taken to drive-by interviews in the hallways. The questions always start out harmless and quickly escalate from there.

How does it feel to be an overnight star?

Is there any way you can top last week's performance against Hillsdale?

Okay, so what is with the fairy dust trend?

Is there any connection between the glitter and the rumors you've tried alternative performance supplements?

Have you heard directly from the VHSL?

As usual, I keep an eye out for Lani in the halls, although it is hard to see anything with my glittery swarm of fans. Like the football guys, ever since the dunks when the guys saw the glitter on my shoes, it's become cool for sports guys and everyone else to slather art store glitter all over their legs and faces. The principal is supposedly cracking down on this "glitter situation," but there isn't much that can be done.

I should be enjoying my last week of being The Bolt. But I sort of want a normal life again. I mean, for one, it's impossible for me to get anywhere on time. Also, there's the issue of me being a fraud. Oh, and Lani. The one person I wanted to impress most—the girl who picked pizza toppings off my shirt when everyone else laughed—could not care less about my athletic feats.

I send her a few vague texts. Desperate texts. She doesn't respond, not that I blame her, I'm sure by now Preston has fed her a bunch of stories about me. Or maybe the truth—which might be worse.

Instead, I find McKenzie Cooper waiting for me at my locker. "Hey Colt, congrats on getting selected player of the week."

"Uh, thanks." I give her a smile. Her blue sweater looks custom made to match her eyes. She leans closer, and I can't help but take a step back. Her minty chewing gum burns my eyes.

The attention is flattering and all, but Lani is the one I like. Doesn't matter though, because just when I thought things couldn't get much stranger, the universe proves it's not done surprising me. McKenzie takes a look around, then gushes, "So, I had no idea Zach was such an athlete."

My locker catches my fall. "What?"

"Yeah, wow. He was doing flips down the hall today." She bites her lip, smiling. "I was thinking maybe he could help out with the cheerleading squad."

You've got to be kidding me.

And this is when Lani happens to walk by, just as McKenzie leans over to me and touches my arm. "Could you, like, ask him to drop by practice after school, maybe?"

"Yeah, sure." I look up. "Oh, hey Lani." The bell cuts me off.

I start after her when McKenzie spins off, making sure everyone hears her say, "See you later, Colt."

And Lani is gone.

After school I haul butt to the auditorium. I want to straighten things out. With Lani. With Mr. Worsham. And yes, even with Preston. I find Lani backstage, sorting through the wardrobe. Of course, Preston and Jennifer and everyone else are standing around too, pretending not to eavesdrop.

"Hey Lani." She glances up and it catches my breath, because her hair is braided into two perfect ropes and she really does look like a princess.

"Oh, hey Colton, what are you doing here?"

It's a fair question. One that gets people looking. Preston fiddles with a button on his stupid gypsy vest. I avoid eye contact with him, but at the same time, I've been thinking about something. I mean, like Jada, what exactly can he say? Is he really going to go around telling people I have magic glitter?

I turn back to Lani. "What do you mean?"

"Well, didn't you quit the play?"

"I did, I mean," I shake my head. "I don't know, I just..." Another look at Preston, who's making zero effort to hide his enjoyment. He cocks an eyebrow, like a warning. I shake my head. "Can I talk to you in private?"

Lani looks confused. "Um, okay."

We step out to a small hallway off the stage, and just as soon as we're alone, all those things I was going to say leave my head. Lani turns and faces me, her fingers playing with a bracelet on her wrist, waiting for me to say something. Only I've got nothing. I rub my hands together and start sputtering. "So, about the play."

She takes a breath. I think about the lake, how she said yes. She said yes before all of this. I try again. "Okay, I mean, I really should have—"

Mr. Worsham is standing in the doorway, the glow of the single bulb hanging above his head like a yellow aura. "All right people, let's move it. Ah, Mr. Clutts. To what do we owe the pleasure of this visit?"

Great. I glance at Lani, realizing that she is waiting for me to say something. "Mr. Worsham, look, uh...it's just that—"

Lani crosses her arms. Mr. Worsham lets me squirm. Finally, I look at my feet, trying to figure out what means more to me. Those stadium cheers, the whistles and chants, the high fives in the hallway? Or Coach Jackson's way. Making a commitment and sticking with it.

Mr. Worsham clears his throat. "Mr. Clutts. To pull off a production, any production, it requires an absolute commitment from those involved. We rely on this commitment to make sure that we all know our places and our lines on opening night. Do you understand?"

I look to him, then to Lani, who stares at me, her eyes piercing my conscience until I have to turn away. Finally, I nod.

"Very well. Now, if you will excuse us, we have little time to get this right. Also, I will need any stage props to be returned. Understood?"

I was so close. "Sure, Mr. Worsham."

With some time to kill before practice, I wander over the hill to the tall grass on the other side of the football field. Even though it's early October I spot some wildflowers in the midst of all the weeds and fast food bags and trash. I pick a few of the purple ones, some reds and blues. Then a few more as the traffic sweeps past below.

A whistle in the distance. From my place on the hill I have a great view of the Peakland Middle football field. Coach Jackson and the guys are down there, getting ready for kickoff. Only a few heads in the stands. Trayvon on his crutches. Phillip and the rest of the guys hopping in place, ready to go. I scan the bench, finding my spot where I'd spent the first two games. Only a week has passed since Coach Jackson yanked me in the Hillsdale game. And everything has been unbelievable ever since.

I bundle up the wildflowers and wait on Lani. And what's funny is that for once I really don't care what people think about it. How I look out here picking flowers. I'm just doing something I want to do.

Thankfully, Lani exits the auditorium alone. I hop to my feet and nearly fall directly on my face because my foot was asleep from sitting cross-legged. She slows when she sees me stumbling around with a makeshift bouquet, then continues out towards the parking lot where I hobble over to catch up.

"Hey," I manage, because I'm that original. I hold the flowers out to her. They've wilted some and the stems are bent and wet from my sweaty hands, but there are a couple of good ones still in there. Her eyes narrow, but the hint of a smile finds the corners of her mouth.

"Look, I just want you to know I'm sorry."

She leans over and picks through the blooms, her nose scrunching up her freckles when she sniffs them. She looks at me and I realize I'm hopping on one foot, trying to shake out the pins and needles.

Lani smiles. "A new training program or something?"

"What? Oh, uh no, my foot's asleep."

She snorts and we start for the parking lot when she stops picking through the flowers and turns to me. "Can I ask you something?"

"Yeah, anything."

"I mean, I never thought you were big into... I don't know." She glances to the direction of the football field. "It's so stupid, the trends people follow."

"What do you mean?"

She rolls her eyes. "I mean, I'm guessing you had that glitter on you because of the play or something. But now the same people who used to make fun of us are wearing glitter. It's kind of ridiculous."

I nod. "Agreed."

Lani looks at me suspiciously. "No really, have you seen Bear and Boar? Or that Porkchop guy? Of course you have, they come over here to escort you to practice."

Porkchop has started carrying a wand around. It's ridiculous. We bust out laughing. Lani with the real gut laughs I've missed so much. "Oh my gosh. They look like a raver nightmare." She sets her backpack down and takes a seat on the bench, still holding the flowers. I sit beside her. She doesn't move away. I take that as a good sign.

"Porkchop has tights, too."

"Stop it. He does not."

"The other day he showed up wearing them. Coach Hudson had to make him take them off. How funny would it be to see Bear and Boar squeezed into my fairy wings?"

Lani pulls out a purple flower. She carefully tucks it behind her ear and looks at me, squinting into the evening sun. "*Your* fairy wings? You quit the play, remember?"

Ouch. "Yeah, I guess you're right."

We let that sit for a while, until she swings her feet a few times then nudges me. I bite my lip, looking out to the passing traffic across the parking lot. Finally, I shake my head with a laugh. "You know it was all an accident, with the prop and all. Abby was playing with it. Then it spilled in my locker, and then..."

Whoa. I have to get a grip, because I almost let it go right there in the school parking lot that my sister had accidently come up with a spell. Twice. And now she's too cool to be much help at all.

"So you spilled glitter on yourself," she says, waving her hands over the parking lot. "And the rest is history."

I laugh. "Yeah, something like that. Look, Lani, about the play, it's—"

Lani shakes her head, hops down, and adjusts her bag. "I'm over it, Colt, really. You've got football, super stardom. All of your glittery football fans now. You don't have time for the play, or the lake. I get it. It's okay, really."

"No. I don't care about any of that." For some reason I remember this morning, in the hallway with McKenzie and how it might have looked. "Oh, about McKenzie, there's nothing going on."

She stares out to the parking lot, then turns to me. "You know what, Colt? You were the only guy who had the courage to be a fairy in the school play." She tosses a strand of hair from her face. "The only one. And even when you fell off the stage and people were calling you fairy boy, you just laughed it off. That's why I said yes when you asked me to the lake or whatever. I thought it was cute how you never took yourself too seriously."

She gathers her things as a minivan approaches. "But now it's like...I don't know, I guess I just didn't realize how much it mattered to you."

I'm about to plead my case when the van stops. Mrs. Andrews waves to me and I'm dazed as I wave back. All I can say is, "More coats?"

Lani turns back to me before she climbs in. "Blanket and food drive at the animal shelter. We're headed to the Humane Society now," she says, looking back at the van. She holds up the flowers. "Well, thanks for these. And good luck with your game this week. Be careful out there, okay?"

Then she's gone. Off to do more good for the world. And the worst part of it all is how she sounds completely over me. I watch the van pull away as I sit alone with the breeze and some wilted flower petals, I realize maybe my wildest dreams weren't so wild after all.

I've spent the past three years crushing on Lani Andrews. And now Colt the Bolt has blown his chance.

Chapter 25
Cold Turkey

At 0-3, Sterling High is what Coach Jackson would call a trap game. Sure, Sterling shouldn't pose much of a threat for a team who's just knocked off Hillsdale. A team that's now 3-0 and sitting atop the Blue division. But again, I can hear Coach Jackson warning about a letdown. And Coach Hudson must know it too, because he isn't about to take it easy on us.

We run play after play, until we have it down. Everyone knows their place and the team is in sync. There is, however, one big uh, glaring problem. Mainly, that I suck. Big time.

Practice is bad. Bad. Bad. Bad.

First, I fall on my face during warmups. Merely bending over to stretch proves dangerous for old Cold Cuts. Actually not on my face. I fall into the broad backside of Bear Davis.

I stumble my way up and down the football field. On a play designed for me to roll out and make a quick pass to Kelvin, I fumble the snap. When I go to pick it up I kick the ball off of Boar's butt and the defense dives on it.

Coach blasts the whistle. "Colt, take it easy son, what are you doing?" The whistle bounces on his lips, whistling with every S.

I smack my helmet with both hands. Coach lines us up to try again. This time I hang onto the snap but the toe of my shoe catches a clump of grass and down goes the quarterback. Again. And that's when the laughing starts.

Coach hits the whistle again. "Colt, come here, kid, What's going on with you?"

"Nothing, Coach, I'll get it, I just..."

Coach Hudson glares at an assistant. One who looks equally stumped. "Maybe he's just a gamer?"

Coach Hudson swivels back to me. "Is that it? You're just saving the good stuff for the game? Or is all that Mr. Panther stuff going to your head?"

The guys laugh. "Um no, not that. I'm saving it for the game." Sure, yeah, whatever. I'm saving *something* for the game all right.

From there it only gets worse. I tumble, stumble, or fumble on every play. We run a rollout play three more times before I get a pass off. An interception. Coach shakes his head, yells for Shane to get in there. Tells me to take five. Gladly.

I find the bench where Zach rushes over, taking a seat beside me. "Dude, you're not looking too hot out there."

"Tell me about it."

He looks at the two hunks of iron that are my feet. My friend seems...lighter today, all put together. It's then I remember the strange encounter with McKenzie. Upon closer inspection, I notice his feet glowing. "Zach, did you, um, play with the recipe again?"

A big smile breaks across his face. "I did it, Colton." He looks around. "Well, Abby did it. I talked her into it. One batch for you, one for me. She'd torn out a page in her little book. Stuffed it in the drawer. But you know what, Colt, you can't stuff away this charm of mine. It's a weapon of mass seduction."

I bury my head. "Please stop."

"And guess what? You're looking at the newest, and only, male member of the cheerleading team."

"What?" My head springs up. This is no good. I have to warn him. "Zach, I wouldn't—"

Before I can get the words out, he's off, handspringing down the sidelines. I get to my feet as my best friend goes end over end before springing into the air. Way into the air. Zach, the guy who gets winded playing video games, does three crazy flips before landing on his feet like he's just hopped off a curb.

Wow.

Practice comes to a halt. Coach and all the guys gawk at Zach like gym class after my dunks. He takes a bow, looking at me as though to say, "Not bad, huh?"

Again, I have to try. I call out to him. "Zach, you don't want to do this."

Zach waves to the guys on the field, then turns to me. "Yes, Colton. I do. And you should be happy for me. You've had the spotlight long enough. Looks like you've got some competition now."

"Zach!" I start after him but it's no use. Besides, I trip over my helmet and go down on my chin. Meanwhile, my best friend goes flipping up the hill like an Olympic gymnast.

At some point practice resumes. I sit on the bench, watching but not watching, wondering what I can do to stop this runaway situation. The sun drops behind the tree line. The vial of magic glitter sits there for the taking, just daring me to dab some in my shoes and get back to business.

Abby did it.

I pick it up, weigh my options. I look out to the field and think of all those things I've done. All the things I could still do. It's right here in the palm of my hands.

All I have to do is use it.

Chapter 26
The Unicorns

"Uh, Colt, there's a small house on wheels pulling into our driveway."

Mom sips her coffee, looking out the living room window. Max jumps when I hop up from my place at the dinner table. Sure enough, a monster-sized suburban is idling in the driveway.

"Well, I guess I'm not walking to school."

"I'm not sure how I feel about this. I mean, you are in middle school."

Abby makes an appearance. It still takes some getting used to, her hair up, her wearing bright girly colors. Asking Mom for a phone, or not wearing those fingerless black gloves I'd always seen her with.

"Good morning, Abby."

"Hmm." She grabs a piece of toast and makes her way back upstairs. Max crawls out from under the table with a stretch. He gives a half-hearted growl to the suburban in the driveway but decides to go looking for crumbs instead.

I tried talking to Abby last night. About the glitter. All she'd say was that she thinks it's wrong but she knows I'll get clobbered out there without it. So that was why she made more. But why make a batch for Zach? She said she's not proud of herself. The dimples made her do it.

I had no words after that.

Two honks from the Suburban and Mom waves. The other day Bear had said no Peakland High quarterback should be caught dead walking to school. I told him I wasn't yet thirteen, that I was okay with it, but he said it wasn't a debate. And when a guy called Bear says you're not walking, you're not walking.

A blast of bacon and Doritos hits my nostrils as I climb into the Suburban. My feet disappear into a cluster of fast food bags and burger wrappers. I turn around and find the rest of the offensive line, all wide-shouldered and two to a seat, stuffing their faces with biscuits. And every single one of them is covered in glitter. Not like a dab on their socks—although they had that, too—it's in their hair, on their arms, all over their jerseys. Big, smelly, 260-pound fairies. It's like they've been lowered into an enormous vat of sparkles. Just a glittery mess.

"Colt the Bolt." Bear greets me with a cinderblock-sized hand on my shoulder. I'm about to say something to the effect of "good morning" when he cranks up the death metal as we back out of the driveway then whips the car into gear.

I guess it's a bad time to mention my dad's war on speeding. But it's a testament to the strength and durability of the vehicle how it's able to move so quickly with so much freight.

Bear turns down the music enough to yell overtop of the screaming guitars. "So, what was up with you yesterday, little man? You messing with Coach, throwing all those interceptions? Being goofy out there?"

"Uh, yep, that's it, being goofy."

Bear chuckles. "Yeah, I thought so. Just wanted to kick it with the new mascot, huh?"

"The what?"

"Your friend. The one doing all those crazy backflips. A male cheerleader." Bear shrugs. "People might laugh, but not me. The way I see it, the guy's got it made."

I set my head back into the seat. The seatbelt hangs loosely, stretched from all the big uglies who usually sit shotgun. I tug at the slack until it tightens, then I stop and cut a glance at Bear, another look back to the rest of them. The glitter. It's too much. All I can do is whisper under my breath. "This is nuts."

"Nope. That little weasel is one lucky dude."

At a stop light, Bear mutes the brain-blender noise and looks over at me. "So we got a little wager on how many yards you're going to get tonight."

"Uh, yeah?"

"Yeah," he says, checking the rearview mirror. I almost lose it when he bats his glittery eyelids. "I bet Boar you could break two-hundred yards rushing, if Coach doesn't pull you out at halftime because we're up by twenty."

"I don't think—"

"Dude, you run for a couple hundred yards and I'll happily pay up," Boar rumbles from the back. The light turns green and I hit the seat. Bear looks me up and down. "Hey, where's *your* glitter?"

"Oh, uh, it's in my locker." *With my fairy wand and wings.*

"Cool. So look, we all know you were messing around in practice yesterday," Bear goes on, "and it is good for a laugh. But if you can run like you did against Hillsdale, you should be good for a few miles against Sterling, easy."

"Yeah but, that was—" I think back to the Hillsdale game. The crowd, the chants. Wait until they see what I do tonight.

Bear slams on the brakes at the next light, catching me with his log of an arm. The back shakes with laughter. Boar pipes, "Oh, and don't worry about Scott, we'll take care of him."

"Scott?"

"Yeah, Steadman. Freshman on the JV team. He thinks you're making a move on McKenzie. Don't sweat it though. You just do your thing."

I'm not sure what *my thing* is anymore, but as they drop me off at the middle school, wearing a Peakland Panthers varsity football jersey, it should feel like a dream come true. Ever since I was in grade school I've dreamed of the day I might pull on the shiny blue and white Panther pride. I just never thought it would happen so fast. Or like this.

Coach Jackson and his coach-speak come to mind. *If you skip the steps that take you to the top, you'll have no foundation on which to stand.* And what's even worse is how I know he is right. I'm shaken from these thoughts as Bear slaps my back.

"See you this evening, Bolt."

"Yeah, see you, dude." Boar gets out of the back and takes the passenger seat for the journey across the parking lot. Gotta love those guys.

As they take off, I think back to that day with the pizzas, how the fame and glory isn't all it's cracked up to be. That maybe coat drives and fund raising, making sure puppies and kitties stay fed and warm, is more important than a stadium full of people chanting your name.

I find McKenzie waiting at my locker. Her shiny blonde hair bounces with her steps and her blue eyes brim with trouble. But I will say this, she wears the glitter much better than the football team.

"Hey, Colt," she gushes. "Where's Zach?"

She's nearly frantic, eyeing up and down the hallway. It dawns on me that I should've stopped by his house instead of riding with the fellas. "Oh, I'm not sure. Hey, is it true about him on the cheerleading squad?"

Her eyes pop wide. Or, wider I should say. "Oh my gosh. Yes. He's so amazing!"

I feel like I'm on the other side of a dream. I can't wake up. Big, burly football players wearing glitter. McKenzie Cooper getting ditzy over Zach. A quick scan of the hallway, everyone is watching me, lots of smiles and fist pumping. This is really happening.

McKenzie touches my arm. "Look, I gotta run. Tell him to find me at lunch, okay?"

I shut my locker. "Yep. Sure will, McKenzie."

Looks like old Scott Steadman is going to have his hands full.

"...*Colt the Bolt...Colt the Bolt...Colt the Bolt...*"

I can't help rolling my eyes. But Principal Morton fights through the crowd, making a beeline for me. I'm about to fall over laughing because he's wearing a dose of glitter himself. Wow. Just wow.

McKenzie smiles, joining in with the chanting. I feel the urge to run away, maybe even get out of the school. It's become too much—the chanting, the cheering. I throw an arm into my book bag strap and duck away. And the funniest part? I don't think they even notice.

I skip lunch and head to the gym where the cheerleaders are busy setting up for the after-school pep rally. Since Peakland Middle beat Sterling, the idea is to band together and support their very own Bolt—me—as I get ready for my second high school start.

A quick peek through the doors. Sure enough, there's my best friend, wearing a saggy track suit, going over his form. An odd mix of envy and happiness stirs in my chest. I mean, yeah, I like Lani, but to see the entire cheerleading team rapt with wonder, hanging on my best friend's every word, it's hard to swallow.

It's like watching a movie where all the characters are clueless. Worse still, I hear Coach Barber is special ordering glitter by the truckload. He wants me to speak at the pep rally, get the crowd going, talk to the local news media. But I'm still ducking Jada.

Up is down, down is up. Lani and I made jokes about it, but the truth is if I put on a tiara and wore a poofy dress, Bear and Boar and the rest of them will follow. Maybe we can change the school mascot to a unicorn.

Chapter 27
Special Effects

At lunch I sneak across the parking lot where every car is covered in glitter dust. *Colt the Bolt* banners line the fence. Fairy wings adorn the columns leading up to the front steps. I need to get away. And there's only one place to go.

The heavy doors to the auditorium thunk shut behind me, sealing off all the chaos of the hallways. The darkness swallows me. The silence pulls me in. The tiny lights guide me down the aisle as my footsteps pad along with my heartbeat as I approach the stage, clutching my beloved props: fairy wings, the wand, and the vial of glitter Zach gave me yesterday.

I'd be lying to say I didn't know what keeps calling me back to the auditorium. Sure, it's Lani, but it's also the stage, the theater, the need to prove myself. Maybe it's just the drama, but I can't seem to stay away.

"Mr. Clutts,"

I jump at the sound of my name, using the arm of a chair to keep from hurling myself into the orchestra seats. Again.

Mr. Worsham appears onstage, loafers tapping with his steps. A hard swallow, as I try to scrape up some words.

"Um, Mr. Worsham, I uh..." My thoughts skitter around my head. In the dark I only see the gaunt outlines of his face, but I feel his gray eyes boring down on me. Mr. Worsham says a good stage performer holds the audience captive. I'm held. "I was, I mean—"

He raises his hand. "Mr. Clutts, I think your biggest

problem is trying to say too much all at once. Now, take a breath. Collect your thoughts."

My thoughts. I want nothing to do with the glitter anymore. I'm done being a fake. A really amazing, super-fast, wildly coordinated fake, but a fake nonetheless. That's what I want. It must be, because I'm here.

I take a breath and set the props onstage. Then I take a step back. The stage lights burn a sunset orange over the drama director's head. "Ah yes, the props."

A smile curls his lips, getting lost in the wrinkles. A chill wiggles down my back.

"Is there anything else, Mr. Clutts?"

All that's left is to turn around and leave. Scamper off and be done with it. Only the hum of machinery over our heads. On cue, the air unit kicks off and all is silent. I look around the empty auditorium. The red cloth seats, the small balcony in the back. The magic of the stage. Man, I really do like drama. And I really want back in the play.

"Mr. Worsham, about the fairy dust. My friend Zach, well, it began with my sister Abby, she..." What's the use? It will never make sense. "Anyway, we sort of messed with the vial."

He tilts his head, his clothes hang on his tall frame like a hanger in the closet. "Messed with?"

I take a breath. "It's kind of a long story."

I'm half expecting him to go into the whole Preston speech about school property. Instead—and no one will ever believe this—he taps his loafers and waves his hands over the seats. The lights go from yellow to pink to purple.

"Whoa." I look around, half expecting to find the stage crew giggling.

"Mr. Clutts, the props, like a performance, have the ability to become magical when taken seriously."

I shake off the chill, taking a step towards the stage.

Carefully I climb up and sit on the edge, just near where I fell. "And if they're not? Taken seriously?"

He grimaces. "Colton, sometimes we get so caught up in the flash we forget what is real and what is not. And sometimes, the success we perceive in our minds, is not, actually, what we most desire."

I scratch my head. Where my dad has his office speak and Coach Jackson has his Coach's speak, Mr. Worsham has this, riddle speak.

"Yeah, I guess so. But the fairy dust, it's, my sister came up with this spell, and it worked."

My words echo off the walls, out loud for the world to hear. It sounds so far-fetched I can't help but wince.

Mr. Worsham tilts his head. He picks up the vial and it pulses to life brighter than I've never seen it before. It's like a lantern glowing in his hands.

He doesn't even blink, only nods. I lower my voice. "It's how I, well, you know—football and all."

"Ah, I see."

"I know how it sounds. But for once I was able to do something right. Only...I, in the end, I guess I didn't."

Before I can say anything else, Mr. Worsham slides over beside me, still holding the vial of glowing fairy dust. He sits back, looking over the rows of empty seats. "Who says this has to be the end, Colton?"

"What do you mean?"

"You're quite the performer, Colton. The field is your stage and you've lived up to the billing. You hold your audience in your hands. They cheer for you and follow your lead holding their breaths and standing on their toes. I think you show great promise in theater."

"Wait, does this mean I can get back in the play?"

He looks down at the vial, still pulsing away. "And your

sister is quite the witch."

"Was. She's too cool for witchcraft, now."

"That's too bad," he says, and I still can't tell if he's messing with me or not. He sets down the vial and the glow between us is gone. Mr. Worsham sighs. "As for the play, Mr. Clutts. That will be for your peers to decide."

"Like a vote?"

"Precisely."

"Hmm, that's going to be tricky."

I've sort of been a jerk to everyone, left them hanging when I became The Bolt, Mr. Big Football Star. And it cost me any hopes of Lani in the process. Now I have to put all of this potions and spells and curse talk behind me. I only wish I could warn Zach. I don't want the same to happen to him.

"Oh, I think you can persuade them." Mr. Worsham is up, nimbly pacing around again, performing. "You know, we are a very superstitious lot, us theater people," he says. *Clip clop clip clop*, his hands behind his back. "For example, one must exit the dressing room left foot first. And we must never place shoes or hats on chairs or tables in the dressing room. Never speak the last line of a production before opening night." He stops, spins back around and whispers, "And never, ever, quote The Scottish Play in a theater."

No clue what he's talking about. I'm still half expecting the wings to sparkle or maybe even levitate. Maybe the wand to float around or disappear altogether. "But we also have short memories."

Mr. Worsham, spry as he is, leans close and snatches up the fairy wings. "And these," he says, holding them with his thumb and index finger, "are simply props."

And that's it.

Chapter 28
Natural Ingredients

I officially withdraw my name from the stupid Mr. Panther contest. It's easy to do, considering I don't even go to Peakland High. Meanwhile, Zach has become a hard guy to track down. He isn't at my locker between classes. Isn't waiting with some crazy new scheme or plan or plots to get a date. In fact, no one is waiting for me, and I get through the rest of the day without being harassed.

After school, a parade comes crashing down the hallways. I catch a blur of Zach doing backflips, leading the way to the gym for the pep rally.

I skip it. Yep, I skip my own big pep rally. I'm no longer in the mood to go out there and pretend to be something I'm not. Instead, I take a walk, eventually heading back across the parking lot, where I end up in the auditorium. This fairy is going to earn his way back into the play.

The doors slap shut and everyone gets quiet. Some whispers and murmuring float in the air as the actors *act* like they aren't making a huge deal about my being there. It's a new sort of calm —peace, even—that comes over me as I waltz down the aisle and take the steps onto the stage. Everyone stares as I find my place at the edge of the semi-circle.

"Well, tonight's the night people," Mr. Worsham announces, roaming the stage with his hands behind his back. The set guys are putting the finishing touches on the altar in the forest. I peek up again at the faces. People whispering. Lani sits at the end with her stage husband, Preston, not only dressing the part now but he's also let his hair go some. He gives me a well-rehearsed sneer and I wink. He's got nothing on me anymore.

Mr. Worsham wraps up the pep talk. I suppose it isn't all that different from the locker room. A bit more elegant, fancy words and accents, but all in all the gist is the same. When he clears his throat, I feel the jitters circulating in my bloodstream. "Finally, we have one other item on the agenda."

I look around, catch Lani's eyes, and she gives me the faintest hint of a smile. Maybe there is hope left in the world after all. Mr. Worsham nods my way.

"Colton here has professed his desire to be back in the play. While personally I'm ready to accept his apology and move on, I thought we could take a vote. So, in the spirit of democracy, I'll let you all decide his fate."

Being theater and all, the process has to be as dramatic as possible. Mr. Worsham passes around a hat. Preston stands, shakes his head, and Mr. Worsham asks if he has something to say. I watch as he opens his mouth, about to spill it about glitter and magic, but then he stops and plops back down.

"Very well."

I study the deep grooves and scratches on the stage as the cast members jot down my fate on torn sheets of paper. I catch a few looks, but mostly they seem like a forgiving bunch. I take deep breaths, tell myself that no matter the outcome, I've done the right thing. I'll probably be in a full body cast after tonight's football game anyway.

Mr. Worsham tallies up the results. I'm reinstated by one vote. I know Jennifer voted for me because she wasn't thrilled being my fill-in. I hope Lani voted for me.

Preston crosses his arms and sulks. Sure, I've broken our deal, but either way it's opening night, and we need to get things moving. Mr. Worsham claps his hands, calling us to action.

"Okay Colton, with your football obligations, you will have a lot on your plate tonight. So you will play your part then be allowed to leave for your game. But Saturday and Sunday, I expect you to be here for the whole production, including encores, if by some stroke of luck, we get through this thing," he says, and suddenly it gets really quiet. "Kidding people, of course we'll get through this."

Then we're off. Prep begins and things get crazy. I wiggle into my tights and reclaim my wings. The vial of glitter sits on the shelf for the taking.

When I come out, I look over to Lani, with her flowery crown and fluttering dress. She catches a glance of me in full fairy costume. It's the first time I've actually worn everything at once and she stops to look me over. I shrug, and she gives me the biggest dimply smile I've ever seen. Then she's off.

Behind the curtains, I go over my lines. A murmur fills the auditorium, the rush of anticipation as this is the real deal. It isn't until I hear the clash of the band somewhere outside that I realize I haven't told Coach Hudson about the play.

But things are moving. Mr. Worsham warns us how opening night never goes according to plan, we'll have to feel out the bumps and weather the storm. Work out the kinks as we go. Without the glitter, there will be bumps, no doubt, and I'm giving myself a pep talk when Zach—a gaggle of cheerleaders trailing behind him—stops by the dressing room to find me in full-on fairy mode. His smirk says it all.

"Um, nice, dude. What is going on?"

"I guess I could ask you the same thing."

McKenzie pokes her head inside. "Um, wow Colt. You look...like a fairy."

"Well, that would make sense," Lani says from across the

room. I stifle a giggle. Sure, I may be a fairy, but Zach, my best friend, is wearing cheerleading pants and a sleeveless Panthers' shirt. And he's draped in glitter. It's a sight.

"Hey, Zach. Can we talk? In private?"

"Uh, sure, but I've got to get down to the field. You should see the banner we've made," he says, smiling at McKenzie. "And just wait until halftime, I've got something extra-special planned."

Because I'm technically still in middle school, the middle school cheerleaders are allowed to tag along for the festivities. As well as all the parents and brothers and sisters and aunts and uncles. "Butts in seats," Coach Hudson calls it. I call it a circus.

Still my loyal hype man, Zach whips out his phone. "Does anyone know you're back in the play. Let me update the feed."

I want to stop him but he's so excited, so worked up. I have no idea how I'll ever bring him back down to earth. He breaks away from McKenzie, who looks me up and down again before leading the cheerleaders up the aisle and out of the auditorium. I motion towards the back door and Zach and I step outside, the low sun hitting our faces. There isn't much time and it's chilly being out there in tights. The trees lining the lot sway with wind.

"Zach. About the glitter."

"Hey man, I'm over it. I'm here for you and I hope you'll do the same for me."

"Yeah, but..."

He grips the railing and looks out over the lot, his bangs flop over his face. He shakes his head then turns to me. "Here's what I want to know. How come when the stuff was working for you, it was all good? But now, since I'm having a turn, getting some of the spotlight, all of a sudden it's wrong. That's lame and you know it."

"Zach, it's not like that. Think about this: what are you going to do when you run out?"

He smiles. I should've known better. Zach the planner. Zach the schemer. "You think I haven't already thought of that? Abby will do it. For me she will."

"It's not real, Zach. You know? Like, did McKenzie ever notice you before you became Mr. Gymnast?"

"She's noticing me now, though, huh?"

"So what happens when you can't do cartwheels?"

"It's a gamble I'm willing to take."

I nod. Fine. If it makes him happy, so be it. "Okay, enjoy it." I look down to my knobby knees in my tights. "But it's probably all over for me tonight."

Zach, watching the rush of cars pouring into the parking lot, smiles. "Well, that was fast. Looks like word has spread about Colt the Bolt being in the play. There won't be one empty seat in there, I'll bet." He rubs his arms. Looks me over. "Wait. What are you saying? You don't mean... You're not, I mean, the football game. You're not thinking of going out there, au natural?"

I shrug.

"Whoa, whoa, whoa. Hang on a sec," he grabs my arm, fully understanding it now, what I'm about to do. "Colt. The play is one thing. But the football game? You can't. I mean, seriously, you can't."

"I'm done with it, Zach. All of it."

His head falls. "Oh man, Colt. Do you know how bad this is going to get?"

The wind snaps to life. A few parents hustle for the door. Behind them, the football rowdies arrive in droves, honking and hooting, decked out with streamers and flags.

The back-door kicks open, knocking me into Zach. I go crashing to the ground. Zach leaps onto the railing. Peter, one of the set guys, finds me on the ground and laughs. "Uh, Colt, we're about to start."

Zach hops down and helps me to my feet.

"Okay, thanks."

Peter turns to go in. I nod to Zach. "Well, wish me luck."

"Dude, this is going to be a disaster."

"Pretty much."

Chapter 29
Break a Leg, or Something

"I s there anyone in attendance who objects to this marriage?" The lights zap and twinkle as I flutter onto the stage—a fairy in the Forest of Contentment. I'm putting my all into the performance, but the football fans are messing up the vibe, hooting and cheering as a huge roar of applause fills the auditorium when I tip out to creep behind Lani and Preston at the altar.

Some idiot shouts, "Colt the Bolt, you're the man!"

I may be done with all the attention, but it isn't done with me. Lani tosses her hair back and powers through it, looking to Preston as I start to cast my fairy spell. They lock hands. All part of the show. More hooting, more chanting. I feel terrible all of my football stuff keeps getting in the way of the play.

It's when I glance up, just for a second, that I get lost in the glare of the stage lights. Considering the vial is safely tucked away with Mr. Worsham, you can probably guess what happens next.

My feet catch and the inevitable ensues. I trip, latching onto the gypsy priest's shoulder but he stumbles back into an already flustered Preston who shoves us upright. Rolling laughter hits the stage. Preston grits his teeth, and it's no act, the guy is furious. I try to spin it as part of my act, but things are getting out of control, and fast.

Disaster averted. Only I'm just kind of standing around, wings glowing and tights, well, tight. I've missed too many rehearsals and forgotten my lines. Poor Lani smiles and tries to coax me along under her breath, but the football fans are now coming down the aisles, some with foam #1 fingers and signs, all of them shouting at the stage.

"We must vanquish this fairy from the forest," Preston says, in his funny accent, trying to power through the mess. I have to give it to the guy, he has dedication. But then, seeing the football fans, and maybe because he's sick of me stealing the spotlight, he launches into his own little improv.

"May you be cast away, fairy boy, be gone with your tights and wings. Flutter along now..."

Some scattered chuckles ring out in the audience, and I feel that familiar tingle of nervousness, just like I'd felt before I tumbled off the stage. The townsfolk stand at the plywood forest, looking offstage to Mr. Worsham for guidance. Lani glances at him, then me with confusion, while Preston mumbles and grumbles before I realize he's trying to spew some kind of curse.

"...that's it now, be gone fairy. Now shoo."

I can't believe he's calling me out like this, right on the stage. But if he wants to improv, so will I. Even if I've got nothing more than nonsense, like those calls I'd used in the huddle.

I go with it, hopping around, flitting and fluttering, waving my wand at him. "Moonlight, stop lights, anchovies and grits. Your breath really stinks and on your nose sits a zit."

His hand flies to his nose. A tsunami of cheers roll onto the stage. Lani covers her smile as the townsfolk double over in hysterics. I didn't want to take attention away from the play, but Preston is the one who ditched the script and started in with the fairy boy stuff. And besides, he really does have a monster-sized pimple on his beak.

He snaps out of his act, turning to the crowd—the crazies with face paint and football jerseys, the parents glancing around trying to figure out if it's all part of the show, the teachers trying to maintain a sense of calm. We probably should close the curtains and save what's left of our play, but that doesn't happen. Nope, things go from great to Cluttstastic.

It all starts the minute I get comfortable. I try to hop back into the forest but crash into a tree and something cracks. Sure enough, Phillip, my favorite video cam guy, leans forward, elbows onstage, grinning big as he catches everything on his phone.

The tree bends back. Another tree sways and the winds of clumsiness take hold of the forest. Another crack. Something snaps. Someone calls out "timber" and the last thing I see is a plywood tree wrench loose with a high-pitched squeak. I look up just in time to see the whole set bend to the left and then...

As it all comes down, I lunge across the stage for Lani and shove her out of harm's way. I get there just in time, moving her towards the curtains. Her flowery crown goes airborne and the twirls of her hair hit my face. The trees crash onto the stage with a boom. Or maybe the boom is the two-by-four crashing down on my back. Ouch. From there I have no idea what else happens because it feels like I'm getting hit by five Kendell Marshalls at the same time.

"Hey, Cold Cuts."

"Ouch."

"Mr. Clutts, are you okay?" Mr. Worsham hovers over me. Zach's head moves in and blocks the lights. When he does I catch a glimpse of Lani, her long eyelashes fluttering, her face struck with concern.

"I think so." I cough. I must have eaten some saw dust on the way down. Miraculously, I'm okay, only a few scrapes on my back.

Mr. Worsham sighs. "Well, the play was an absolute disaster. But you however, can add hero to your growing list of accomplishments."

I sit up, trying to focus. Lani kneels by my side, a hand to her chest and a twirl of her hair touching my cheek. "Colt, you saved my life."

"Well now, let's not get carried away," Preston says, somewhere behind the heads and the lights, his tone pretentious as ever. His boots click with his steps. "I mean, we all could have been hurt. I would have shoved you out of the way if I'd been over there. Besides," he motions to me, "he *is* the one who pulled the thing down in the first place."

"That will be enough, Preston, thank you," Mr. Worsham says curtly. Preston marches off in a huff, but he runs directly into Porkchop Peterson. "Whoa there, pirate," Porkchop chuckles.

"I'm not a pirate," Preston grumbles in defeat.

"Colt, oh colt!" Mom squeezes through the crowd like a running back hitting the hole. She slides to my side and takes my face in her hands. Luckily, I'm too groggy to be mortified.

"Mom, I'm fine. Please."

The auditorium has become a circus. People scrambling to get a closer look, football fans and parents standing and pointing, even snapping pics. Bear and Boar work like bouncers, keeping the crowd at bay so I can have some space.

Mom prods my neck, behind my ears. She's big on acupressure and tension relief. "I can't believe that happened, that thing fell right on your back."

"Yeah, who knew drama could be more dangerous than football?" I look up to see Abby shaking her head, smiling. It's nice to see her smile again.

I look over to Lani and whisper, "Are you okay?"

"Shouldn't I be asking you that?" she says with a laugh.

Then Bear chimes in. "Dude, you going to be able to play tonight?"

With everyone hovering over me I almost forgot my night is only half over. Hmm. I'm actually fine, considering. Still, maybe I can string along this stage injury and not have to play? That's it. I'm injured. Injured being a hero no less! It's kind of perfect.

Kind of.

The crowd starts up with the chanting and stomping, disregarding any sort of theater etiquette. "Colt the Bolt, Colt the Bolt!"

"Oh, the humanity." Mr. Worsham rushes back. I lift my head, realizing I'm not so bad off after all. And if I don't play, the mob will want my head on a stick. Besides, one glance at the Glitter Brothers and I know ducking the game is not an option.

Sure, the football game is a job for Colt the Bolt. And considering how I hardly survived the play, taking the field without the glitter is a march to certain death. But as I get to my feet without help, the crowd eats it up, and hearing my name like that, well, I gotta admit, part of me still believes my own hype. That maybe, just maybe, I can go out there against Sterling and pull it off.

Abby sneaks up to my side. She gives me a once over. I can tell she knows before she leans in, talking under her breath. "Why aren't you using the glitter?"

"It's that obvious?"

She rolls her eyes. "Um, Colt. You just took down an entire production. Only you. Maybe Dad."

"Oh, right. I guess I forgot to tell you. I'm through with the glitter. With all of it." Then I go all big brother on her. "I still can't believe you made it for Zach."

Abby looks down, kicks her feet, blushing. "Yeah, that was

stupid. I mean, I'm over it." Then she gasps. "But Colt, you can't go out there without—"

Before I can say anything else, I'm hoisted up and hauled off the stage by Porkchop Peterson.

"Come on, Bolt. Time to go kick some Sterling butt."

As I'm carted off stage, I look back and find Abby shaking her head. And that reminds me—I reach for my pocket, where I find four jacks.

And for once in my life, I don't throw them away.

Chapter 30
Running Game

When I get to the field, Coach Hudson's face is like that of a tomato in my dad's hands. Red and wrinkled.

"You're late, Holden."

"Colton."

"I heard there was a little accident on the stage. You okay?"

"Well, I don't..." I probably should warn him that he doesn't have a phenom on his hands but an idiot. Because I'm definitely more Colt the *Dolt* than *Bolt*, and whatever dust is left in my shoes is just that, dust. I can still see Abby's face when I told her. And now I'm sort of regretting the whole thing. In fact, I'm terrified. But before I can get the words out, he grabs my shoulders and jostles me around some.

"Good. Now go get warmed up."

We elect to receive. I tie up my cleats and steady my thoughts. *Boom* goes the kickoff. I yank on my helmet and prepare for the end. This is it. It's all over now. The crowd, the news reporters. Jada. Trayvon. In just a few short minutes they will all know I'm a fraud. But I probably won't be alive to see it.

A quick glance to the sidelines. It's clear the newest superstar cheerleader is having his own issues. Poor Zach is a mess, tumbling around, his shirt ripped and grass stains on his knees. It's obvious something is going way wrong for my best friend. He keeps trying, though, his hair flopping as he jumps an inch, trips, then falls on his face. The crowd eats it up, the way they would a monkey at a circus. McKenzie and the rest of the squad look ready to kill, arms crossed and scowling. Wow, clearly this is not going to end well for either of us.

My attention is jolted as Coach grabs me by the facemask. "Okay, you've had a rough week of practice. But I need you to go out there and remind me why you're on this team."

I gulp down a breath and head for the huddle, tapping my cleats out of habit. One last look over my shoulder. Poor Zach is flat on his back. I shake my head. If only he would have listened to me earlier.

A few careful steps as I stumble. I've got the jacks stuffed in my cleats, but my spine feels like an old rope, my mind a wad of petroleum jelly. This is not the way I envisioned leading the Panthers to victory.

Out in the huddle, I try to rally. "Hey guys, what's up?"

Crickets. A few moans maybe. With my sudden superstardom, it never occurred to me how these guys had gotten the shaft. They've actually worked their way to varsity through summer camps and practice and training. I've simply cruised onto the scene and ball-hogged my way to the top. I take a second to set things straight.

"Look guys, I'm sorry. I mean it. I've been a snot-nosed ball hog."

A few facemasks lift. Some snickering. "Hey, Mike." I nod to our running back, Mike Kendrick. I'm embarrassed to say I had to look up his last name. But I'm ready to make amends. "I hope you're ready to run for a couple hundred yards tonight, because we need you."

"You're really going to let someone else touch the ball?" He rolls his eyes. A blast of the whistle. Delay of game. Not this again.

I don't dare look to the sidelines. Instead we back it up and I call the play. "Sweep left, on two." Mike's eyes get big, and I nod to Bear and Boar and the rest of the linemen. "Hey guys, clear the way."

Porkchop nods. "Done."

It isn't the play Coach sent me in to run. He called a bootleg, where I run down the sidelines, burn it up like last week. But I know that if we have any chance of winning (and me living to see another day), it's going to be with the ball in someone else's hands.

It works, Mike busts up the middle for ten yards on first down. I trip on the next play, but manage to get the ball in his gut and he rolls for another fifteen. Suddenly, we're in business. Tackling isn't exactly one of Sterling defense's strengths, and with the wind on our backs I'm content to keep running the ball and rolling up yardage. Sure enough, Mike's legs carry us down the field and we score on our first drive.

My stats: 0-0 for 0 yards. The crowd is no longer just chanting my name but the Panthers, which is kind of nice. Off the field, Coach Hudson nods my way. "Way to read the defense, Clutts."

I smile. A big lead is my only hope. Then maybe I can take the bench and live a long and happy life. No such luck. Sterling High has nothing to lose. They actually go for it on fourth down, twice, then score on a fake punt.

On our second offensive series, Sterling starts to figure us out. Or, figure me out. Our running game stalls, mainly because the defense plugs eight guys in the box, which if you remember is football talk for targeting the scrawny, no-good quarterback. They're basically daring me to pass. Considering my game is fake as Photoshop, I'm not about to take a chance on it.

By our third series, Mike's uniform is more brown than blue and he's hunched over, sucking wind in the huddle. I call a reverse for Kevin, the speedster wideout, and he gets a first down. Then I hand it to our beefy tight end. I do anything but pass, and soon the guys are asking questions.

"What's going on with you, Clutts?"

"Huh, oh, I'm trying to get everyone involved."

Bear shakes his head. "Go score a touchdown and we'll meet you in the end zone. You can 'involve' us there."

Halftime is awkward. I've made it the entire half without a single pass. Just like last game, except I had two hundred yards on the ground by then against Hillsdale. Coach Hudson paces and grumbles, shoots daggers my way. *Gamer my butt,* he's thinking, and honestly, I'm secretly hoping the guy will come to his senses and bench me. But he doesn't. He's waiting for the magic to happen. And thoughts of the old shower stall come to mind.

But I don't have the glitter, just some old playing cards in my shoe. So things only get worse.

In the second half the wind picks up and my noodle arm doesn't stand a chance. In the huddle, I set my hands to my knees, squeezing my pants so the guys don't notice how badly I'm shaking. I turn to Mike, who looks away. I get the feeling he's tired of carrying us on his legs.

Kelvin, who besides the one run has been all but ignored, takes command of the huddle. "Hey shrimp. Look, you going to spread the ball around or what?"

And just like that, I realize I'm going to have to pass the ball.

Chapter 31
Air It Out

It's after my third interception that the crowd finally turns on me. It's funny, but not funny, what a few poor throws can do for your image. Only moments ago everyone was chanting Colt-the-Bolt, all glitter-trocious, bearing signs with my name on them. Now I'm worried about a stampede from the stands.

I remind myself how my dad never had any fairy dust or magic tricks back in his day and he's one of the strongest people I know. He survived high school—in the marching band, no less—then college and was even lucky enough to wind up with Mom.

All of this is swimming in my mind late in the fourth quarter in the midst of a 14-14 tie game. "Okay guys, let's get this score."

Boar looks ready to strangle me. "Can you throw it to the right team this time?"

Fair enough, I'm thinking, still smiling, continuing my first half strategy of staying upbeat and keeping the team with me. Shane stands on the sidelines, hands in his pockets. Coach Hudson motions for me to get going with the play. I guess he's still thinking I've got some magic left. But all I've got is some corny advice from my dad.

Dad says a true leader keeps his wits about him in the face of adversity. Typical office dribble, but it's all I've got at the moment. "Guys, I take full responsibility for—"

The team breaks from the huddle, without me. The Sterling

fans get to their feet. It's almost like they've multiplied as the game has gone on. Now they're bouncing and confident. Can't say I blame them.

Mike scurries right and picks up nine yards but fails to get out of bounds. The clock continues to roll. We're out timeouts because Coach has burned through them so he could chew me out. With under forty seconds left in the game, I can't fathom how all of this happened. I, Colton Clutts, seventh grade doofus, am quarterbacking the Peakland Panthers varsity team. Not The Bolt, *me*.

We line up again. The call is a screen pass to Kelvin. Screens are all I can handle, and just barely. I drop back and sling the ball his way, an ugly floater that's behind him so he has to come back to make the catch and gets nailed for a loss...

tick...tick...tick...

Second and fourteen. We line up in shotgun, run a draw. Mike scampers ahead for fifteen yards. Our side of the stands comes alive. Twenty seconds left. Coach motions like a mad man for us to get moving. I flail my arms, shouting for the guys to line up.

The ball in my hands. A blur of grass and bodies. It feels like the last two weeks—the middle school game, the gym class dunks, Hillsdale, the floaty pass play, Preston, McKenzie, Jada, Zach, Lani—have been tossed in the blender that is my brain.

This is it. I roll back, stumbling, but trying my best to stay upright. An inspired defense rushes me for the kill. They smell an upset cooking. Or my fear—my fear is definitely cooking. Either way, things close fast. I spin one way, then the other, woozy and clumsy, running like a dizzy hamster in a maze. Ten seconds...

Doubling back, the play eats up way too much time. I know I have to make something happen. That's when I find a wide open Mark Burton near the sidelines. But there's no way I could chuck the ball into the wind and across the field. The Bolt? Sure. Me? Not so much.

But the guy is completely alone. He's waving me down, trying to get my attention. Mark's been forgotten as the defense goes all in for the sack. Now, with five seconds left, he's all we've got. I take a few shaky steps, close my eyes, and launch the ball high into the lights just before the giants drill me into the ground.

My lungs empty as I hit the dirt like a sack, hoping I've put enough on the pass. My arm hurts. My head hurts. Heck, my toenails hurt. The crowd oohs and ahhs before one side of the stadium goes bonkers. I roll over to my stomach, exhausted and hopeful.

It's not our side cheering.

By the time I can get my head off the ground, the Sterling safety is prancing down the sidelines. I scramble to my feet, but before I can do much of anything I'm blasted again by a block as the safety dashes into the end zone and the clock shows zeroes.

Touchdown Sterling.

I hang my head, wishing I could dig my own grave right there on the field. Maybe future Peakland teams can start a tradition of walking past my plot and shaking their heads, remembering the worst quarterback in the history of high school. I've just cost us a game we were supposed to win by twenty points. I don't need to look up to see the Sterling players gathering in a pile at the end zone. I can hear it all.

No one comes to help me up. I fall back and lay there, a lump of hopelessness. The hero turned chump, left to rot on the field. Last week's high-flying sensation is this week's puny middle schooler, a flop who's just thrown his fourth interception (well, technically it was a touchdown, just to the wrong team).

I bang my helmet out of frustration. The curse won after all. How could I have ever thought otherwise?

It's in the midst of this misery I notice footsteps behind me. "So me helping you up is kind of like our thing?"

I manage to turn around, where I find a pair of familiar neon green sneakers. Lani?

She starts to help me up but I somehow manage to get tangled in my shoulder pads and it takes a minute to get turned around. Like a dog chasing his tail, I spin a few times before falling down again. Lani watches with amusement as the Sterling crowd rushes the field to join the celebration going on in the end zone. We try again and she helps me to my feet.

I remove my helmet, the night air cold on my sweaty head. "Man, I really blew it, huh?"

She shrugs, jamming her hands into her pea coat. She takes a look around, like it's her first time on a football field. "I guess. We just got here."

"Really?"

She bites her lip. "Actually, we ran the play again after you left, without the set, of course. But we got a standing ovation," she adds proudly. "From the seven or eight parents watching."

"What?" I ask, still dusting myself off. I'm a little jealous. A few Sterling players brush past me, offering me a handshake. I guess I am sort of their MVP. But most of them are classy winners, unlike I had been against Hillsdale.

"Well, I'm glad I wasn't there to mess that up again."

We start off towards the sidelines when Lani stops and touches my arm. "What? No, you were the reason everyone was there. We set a box office record. I can't *wait* for tomorrow's show. And between you and me, Jennifer's *not* the best fairy."

She gives me a smile, one that makes me forget I've just thrown most of my completions to the wrong team. She's still wearing her gypsy bride stage makeup, and her eyes shimmer behind her glasses.

"You mean I'm still in the show?"

She nudges my arm. "Of course you are. And Preston has promised to stick to the script."

Coach Hudson waves me over to the bench, where seeing my teammates, something else enters my mind: I owe Bear like a hundred bucks.

I look at Coach, then to Lani. "Well, I gotta go face my teammates."

"Okay, but hey, we're all going to Michelangelo's for pizza, the cast and crew party. You want to join us?"

"Really?"

"Yeah," she says, making a face. "You *are* part of the cast. Plus, you did kind of save my life and all."

I smile. "Well, that was kind of my fault, too you know. But sure, I'll be there."

"Cool." She turns to walk off, but then spins around and tilts her head, glancing over to the sidelines. "Um, Colton, you probably shouldn't go over there smiling like that."

"Oh, right."

I pull my helmet back on as I approach a bench full of glares. Coach Hudson waves me into the huddle. "Okay team, I won't lie, that was rough out there. But let's remember one thing, we win or lose as a team. No one person is responsible."

Wow, I wasn't expecting him to have my back. And not just him. Mike sets an industrial-sized hand on my shoulder pad. "Coach is right, we all overlooked these guys. I thought we were going to show up and cruise to a win."

Slowly, I raise my head. It appears the team is not going to kill me. My limbs will stay intact. Not just that, but one by one, the guys come over to me and pat me on the back, tell me to keep my chin up.

And so I do.

Chapter 32
Humble Pie

My arms. It's all I can do to pull the door open at Michelangelo's. But one whiff of warm bread from the toasty ovens brings me back to life. On the way over, Dad told me a hundred and two times how he was proud of me. But he left it at that. None of the usual moral victory stuff or office speak. Maybe there is hope for that guy after all.

What a night. I crashed onstage and took out the entire set only to follow it up with an epic stinker of a football game. And yet, as I stroll into the restaurant I find a room full of friends. They break into a standing ovation. Even a few of the more faithful Peakland football fans join in. I take a bow. It's not every day someone is so remarkably terrible as I've just been.

Coach Jackson and Trayvon nod from their table near my old middle school teammates in a corner booth. It's funny, because, looking around, you'd never know that we'd just lost a game we should have won by three touchdowns. First thing I do is escape Dad, who, judging by the misty-eyed look on his face is gearing up for that cheesy speech about moral victories after all.

I'm on my way to Lani and the crew when Zach cuts me off. His arm is in a sling, and to my disbelief, McKenzie stands close to him, seemingly by choice. She looks me over with a pity smile. Zach leans close. "So, I figured out what happened. With my acrobatics."

"Yeah?"

"Abby. I think she un-spelled the glitter."

"Really?" I look around for Abby and Mom, before I realize Abby is probably at a sleepover or movie or doing something normal. Not being a witch. Zach shakes his head, all smiles, with his dream girl by his side. He gives me a salesman's smile.

"Yeah. You know what they say. There's nothing worse than a woman scorned."

"I guess so," I say with a laugh. "Looks like you're doing okay though. I mean, besides the arm and all."

"Yeah," he says. "I got two calls from Olympic coaches. And look, as for you? Well, you think any other quarterback will ever rush for four-hundred yards in a game? Those records are all yours."

"Thanks, Zach." I can't help but laugh. I'm so over it.

"Yep. Hey, come join us when you have some time, superstar. We still have to figure out what to do with two hundred *Colt the Bolt* t-shirts."

I shake my head, watching McKenzie lead Zach over to a booth, where he slides in and rips off a bite of pizza and shovels it in his mouth.

No upperclassmen or cheerleaders. No one chanting my name, and best of all, no glitter. Just good pizza and good people. What's crazy is how the main topic of conversation humming around isn't even the game. It's my tights. With everything going on I hadn't even noticed I'm still wearing them under my football pants.

It's great. All of it. But first, I know what I have to do, which is offer up a big fat apology to the guy who tried to keep me grounded when I had my head in the clouds. The guy who would have been completely justified in saying "I told you so." But that isn't Coach Jackson's style.

I slink over to my old coach, ducking my head, hardly able to look him in the eye. "So, uh, did you save my spot on the bench?"

"Funny you ask. I just got off the phone with Coach Hudson. He thinks you need a few years before you're ready for the big time."

We laugh at the same time. At 3-1, the varsity team's season is still humming along. It doesn't take a genius to figure out I should be back in middle school, riding the pine and learning the basics. Fine by me. I'm done with the spotlight. I nod to my old coach. Not much else to be said.

"See you Monday?"

Coach Jackson shoots me a rare smile. "Sounds good. But hey, you owe me a few laps."

"I owe you a lot more than that."

Trayvon grins, reaches out his hand. "Tough game, man. Keep your head up." He holds up two fingers. "You got to start a varsity high school game, twice."

We take turns laughing about my horrible game, about what Coach Hudson must be thinking. Safe to assume he's done with "phenoms" for the rest of his coaching days.

I scoot away, wandering over to the drama peeps. I pass Preston on the way over and he slides out from the table and stands. *Here we go*, I'm thinking. But he sort of smiles. With a shrug, he waves a hand over me. "I hereby un-curse you."

We both crack up laughing.

"Thanks."

He nods. I nod back. Hey, it's a start.

Carefully, I turn to Lani's table. "Do I know you guys?"

Lani looks up, her wide brown eyes locking me into place. Kirsha and Jennifer exchange giggles. And that's when it dawns on me that I've just approached Lani Andrews without falling or tripping or even stuttering. Huh, maybe I *am* un-cursed. Or maybe it's time to stop thinking about curses.

Lani points to the pizza. "Pineapple?"

I plop down in the seat beside her. "Usually I just toss it on my head."

"You know, self-deprecating humor is something I look for in a guy."

More giggling. My cheeks burn. "Really? Because there's more where that came from. I mean, here you guys are, sitting with a quarterback who has just tossed not one, not two, not even three, but *four* interceptions in just one game."

Lani shrugs. "I don't even know what that means."

Kirsha giggles. "Is that good?"

"Not exactly," I say with a laugh. "Oh but hey, I was giving some thought to my lines in the play. I think they should all be raps."

A collective groan. Lani gestures to the table. "We think you should stick to the script."

"Okay, fine. I guess no one appreciates a well-versed, rapping fairy anymore."

Lani looks over my shoulder and frowns. "Oh, Colt. I'm sorry Zach stole your girlfriend."

Across the room, McKenzie Cooper fawns over my best friend, even helping him fix his sling. Zach is eating it up. I turn back to the table. "I think I'll manage. She isn't exactly my type."

"That's good to know," Lani says with a wink. More giggling around the table. I reach for a slice of pineapple pizza. Lani steadies my hand. "Careful."

Chapter 33
Once a Witch...

That night, with my fifteen minutes of fame and shame all used up, I hit the bed and fall sound asleep in seconds, snoozing until sometime after nine the next morning when I'm awakened by my dad tumbling off the ladder outside my window.

I roll out of bed and roam to the kitchen where Abby is writing in her new pink diary, bugging Mom about a family data plan.

"Well, it's alive," Mom says with mock astonishment. I rub my ear. I must have slept on it wrong again.

"Sort of," Abby says, sipping tea like the mini adult she's become. She slips down into her chair at the table. "So, what's in store for tonight? Are you going to set the stage on fire?"

I grab the Captain Crunch. "Hey, I need to ask you about—"

Abby shoots me a look, shakes her head, which sort of tells me everything I need to know. Mom leans her head back in. "About what?"

"Oh, nothing. Just something about how I have the greatest sister in the world."

Mom's eyes go wide. "Okay, well *now* I know something's up." But she walks out, giving us some privacy.

I bring my bowl to the table, talking low. "So, you un-spelled a spell?"

Abby blows on her tea, shrugs, and tries to hide her grin. "Maybe."

"So, I'm done with the glitter, are you done with the spells?"

The grin widens. "Probably."

"*Probably?* That doesn't sound promising."

"Well, never say never, right? I mean, especially when I can do so much."

For a minute I see stars in her eyes. Oh boy. My spoon clinks against the bowl. "Abby."

It's too late. She sets her tea down, narrows her eyes. It's then I catch a glimpse of what's in her diary. Moon phases, herbs, potions, and spells. She slaps it shut. "Think about it, Colton. I can do so much with this... I can stop bullies, fight crime. Maybe do something about climate change. I can... Oh my gosh, Colton. I can change the world!"

"And here I just want to get through the day without falling on my face."

Mom returns and we go silent. I catch sight of the newspaper on the table. I reach for the sports section but Abby beats me to it, snatching it up and walking away.

"Hey!"

"Sorry bro, but you really don't want to read that."

"Well, *now* I do."

She glances at Mom, who nods. Abby sighs then hands it over. "Just don't take it personally, this paper is a rag."

I unfold the sports section and read the headline,

"Phenom" Quarterback Tosses Four Picks in Loss to Sterling.

I look at Mom and Abby. Pretty bad. But I expected as much.

Colt Clutts, the middle-school quarterback who led the Panthers to an improbable victory over the Hillsdale Cardinals last week, looked thoroughly lost in last night's stinker.

Wobbly and unsteady all night, he showed no sign of the magical moves from last week, which Sterling Coach Waverly credited to his defense.

I set the paper down and laugh until I'm leaking milk through my nose and Abby is calling me gross, but then she breaks out laughing too. Pretty soon, Mom is cracking up, and I go back and read the best parts out loud.

Coach Hudson may want to have his quarterback's eyes checked, after several passes were lobbed to the guys in the wrong jersey.

By the time Dad swings through the door, dusting leaves from his head and muttering about the strength and design of the ladder, we've all lost control. He sees us with the paper and joins in on the fun.

At times he looked like a frightened chicken...more scrambled than scrambling...

We sit around the table, having a good laugh at my expense. Just like old times.

THAT NIGHT our play goes on in front of a half empty auditorium. It's amazing. All the rowdy football fans stay home, leaving mostly parents and a couple of students who actually *want* to watch a forgetful play in attendance. No foamy #1 fingers in the seats. It's nice.

Sunday's performance is even better. We have things down and we're clicking. We receive a standing ovation, and I even take the stage with the cast for an encore. Mr. Worsham said it was one of his finest moments as a director, and I kind of got the feeling he says that every year. But still, it was pretty cool.

Lani and I hang out almost every day after school. She's moved on to another production while I've gone back to middle school football practice. I've even joined her for a coat drive and to clean kennels at the local humane society. I still haven't told her about the curse or the spell and I'm not sure that I ever will. Where would I begin?

Overall, going back to being seventh-grade scum isn't so bad. Although Zach is crushed. McKenzie patched things up with Scott. We've moved back to our little lunch table, but he did manage to sell those shirts, and every now and then I pass some hipster wearing the irony that is a *Colt the Bolt* shirt and I just laugh.

As far as football, the middle school guys welcomed me back. With two varsity games to my credit, they look to me like a seasoned pro. Even still, I made a formal apology to the whole team, told them how sorry I was for being a bucket head when I got all big-time. Porkchop Peterson still checks in on me occasionally, and my records still stand across the lot over at Peakland High.

I did, after all, run crazy all over Hillsdale and set all sorts of state records before my implosion against Sterling. Coach Hudson says he'll save a spot for me in a couple years. We'll see.

I think a lot about that special night against Hillsdale. How I played, the magic, the pass that seemed to hang in the air. People around town still argue about it. Dad says the old timers in the stands still haggle over whether there was a string on that ball. Jada has moved on, although she still likes to bring up that rulebook every now and again.

As for Abby, I think Mom enjoys the shopping sprees and girl talk. She finally got her own iPhone (after another round of straight A's my parents were left with no choice). But I can tell she's up to something. I saw it in her eyes at breakfast when she was talking about changing the world. It was in the pages of that little pink diary. It's written all over her face as she flips through a deck of cards. I know what she's thinking. She may say she's changed, but I'm not buying it. Because I know the truth.

My sister is a witch.

LOOKING FOR MORE?

Turn the page for an exclusive sneak peek at *Spellbound*, the exciting sequel to *Fairy Dust Fumble*.

Coming in October 2022 from Immortal Works.

SPELLBOUND

CHAPTER 1

It's mayhem outside of Peakland Middle School. Stampedes
bust through the exits, and kids scatter in all directions. Some
flee toward the parking lot, others seek the safety of the football
field or farther still, the abandoned railroad tracks in the nearby
woods. One boy has climbed the flagpole.

A mass evacuation is in order. This is not a test.

The schoolyard is a battlefield of debris. Notebook paper,
textbooks, book bags, discarded masks, hall passes, gym towels,
an abandoned tennis shoe—at least one tuba—litter the grounds.
Those who haven't fled huddle in chattering groups near the
pick-up lane, eyes are wide and abuzz after the early dismissal
was issued.

A line of honking minivans and SUVs snake around the
school parking lot, slowing only enough to allow kids to hop in
before they go screeching out of the lot before the door can even
be shut.

I can't help the swell of pride that finds my chest, although
this is no time to enjoy my handiwork. My two best friends,
okay, *only* friends, Chuck Tinsley and Ahmad Das stand loyally
by my side, taking in the scene on this otherwise sunny and
warm fall day. I wipe my hair back, wondering whether I've
gone too far or haven't done enough.

The moment is short-lived, zapped like a pulled plug when
my brother comes charging through the crowd, making his way
toward me. I take a breath and hold my eye roll. Colton's not in
a rush because he's worried about my safety, that I can assure
you. He's on to me, but I expected as much, even from him.

Sure enough, here he comes, to chide me like a disobedient dog. "Abby." His face is flushed, his eyes scan the grounds. "Abby. You need to fix this, fast."

"Oh Colton, I'm so glad you're safe." I launch into him with a hug, figuring I might as well sell it.

He shoves me off. I smile for Chucky and Ahmad's benefit —they're looking a bit skittish—when Colton spins me around by the shoulder and lowers his voice. "Abby, you promised."

First of all, I did no such thing and he knows it. Still, I set a hand to my chest, ducking away from him because his breath smells like pork rinds. "Whatever do you mean?"

Behind me, Chuck giggles. Neither he nor Ahmad have any idea what's happening, but I have their support. Blind loyalty such as theirs is hard to find these days. If you can find yourself a couple of quiet friends, ones who will stand at your side through the best and the worst, keep them close. It's probably their biggest asset.

Colton shoots Chucky a stern look that shuts him down. "This isn't funny, Chuck."

Greenie, the hall monitor/parking lot attendant, comes shoving through the crowd. He's Code Red frantic today, his stringy hair out of place, his eyes loose in their sockets as he wields a forehead thermometer like a gun. The early dismissal clearly has him unnerved—which isn't saying a lot as far as Greenie is concerned. Under normal circumstances Greenie is only a hall pass away from a breakdown. Now, with a couple hundred kids gathered on the curb, the lawn, the sidewalks, left to mill about without order—well, he's never going to make it.

He fights through the madness, shaking the beeping thermometer, shooing people into place, shouting orders:

"Single file!"

"Away from the curb."

"All right, all right, no pushing or shoving."

"No yelling."

"You! Come here, now!"

"Hey, who spit chewing gum on the sidewalk?"

Poor Greenie. It's his worst nightmare come to fruition. And I know all too well about living-nightmares. It happened to me a mere two months ago, when I left out an "R" in "embarrass" during the final round of the national spelling bee. Talk about irony.

Greenie's voice cracks, and the sweat patch on his back looks like a world map. I watch him scurry about, bending over to examine a sock, when Colton waves for my attention.

He lowers his voice. "Abby, it's just that..." He looks around, checking to make sure no one is paying attention. They're not, how could they? Not with the ambulance hitting the siren twice as it pulls out onto the street. "We said no more spells."

No more spells. *Oh* the nerve. The spell thing only began last year after he was cast as a fairy for a school play. I was messing around with his props—wand, wings, glitter—and stumbled across something that worked. Next thing I knew, he was doing all sorts of crazy things on the football field—running, jumping, zipping around. He set high school football records even though he was only in the seventh grade. And now, because things didn't end so well for him, he's going to tell me right from wrong? Please.

"Abby."

"What?"

"No more spells," he repeats, looming over me, waiting for me to buckle.

Ridiculous. Here I have the power to stop evil. I can right wrongs, small and large. I've discovered a way to single-handedly balance the power between the strong and the weak.

And I'm supposed to stand to the side and watch, turn the other cheek, betray those in need? No thanks.

I shrug and pat him on the shoulder. "Relax, bro."

He looks at my hand, then me. "Bro?"

I roll my eyes. Sometimes, with Colton, you have to s-p-e-l-l things out. Or you fix things, sit back, and let him think he's making the call. "It should wear off by nightfall."

His eyes bug out. "So it *was* you?"

"Duh." I sigh, looking around. A faint *thump thump thumping* overhead.

"And what do you mean, *should* wear off? Please tell me Chaz Snead will be okay."

"Fine. It *will* wear off. Stupid Chaz will be completely fine. And hopefully he will have learned a very valuable lesson."

The news station chopper makes a fly over. Hmm, I have to admit, I wasn't planning on this much media attention. However, Mr. Wolff, our new principal, doesn't seem rattled in the least. In fact, he's especially calm, walking among us with his hands clasped behind his back as he checks on students, parents, and staff with a creepy big smile on his odd face.

A crash out in the street steals my attention from Mr. Wolff. A minivan has rear-ended an SUV. Traffic on Eastwood grinds to a halt. Police cars, sirens, the news—it's all a bit much. But sometimes that's what it takes for a bully to learn a valuable life lesson.

Yes, I did it. Because Target #1, Chaz Snead, has terrorized Peakland Middle school without consequence for far too long. He goes after the short, the weak, the quiet, the, *ahem*, moderately average. Google "Bully" and Chaz Snead appears amidst a string of algorithms and keywords. Just last week he dumped cayenne pepper in Morty Grabowski's gym shorts. But long before that, I'd decided Chaz Snead was no good, and he deserved what he got. The algorithm has changed.

Hmm, I like the sound of that.

Honestly though, I might have left him off my list had he not started in with Chuck. I have a weakness for underdogs. And Chuck, with his corduroy pants and off-brand tennis shoes, is like a runt under a porch. So the other day when Chaz called Chuck "Splotch," then "Smear," referring to the birthmark on my friend's cheek (I think it's shaped like Italy), it got my attention. And when Chuck's lip started quivering like he was going to start crying in class, well, Chaz Snead found himself at the top of my newly formed hit-list.

That was the day he became Target #1.

And now, having put Chaz in his place, Colton is telling me to knock it off? The nerve. Funny how things change. Again, the nerve, I tell you.

Looking out to the street, I watch parents argue over right-of-way and signals. It's remarkable how frightened everyone looks, almost comical, how easy it is to shake up routine and ruin these fragile mental states. But they shouldn't be scared, so long as they behave like decent human beings.

But where there is a Target #1, there is a Target #2, and a #3.

Oh, these mortals. Don't they realize what I can do? No, they don't. And that's why it's so hard to keep the smile from splitting my face.

A few hours ago this was a mundane school day. I was eating with Chuck and Ahmad. It was a rare occasion, my two closest friends hardly ever eat lunch anymore because Chaz always does *something* obnoxious to *someone* in the cafeteria where he has an audience. I assured them both all was fine, everything was taken care of, when sure enough, Chaz strolled by and said, "Hey Smear," to Chucky, all the while oblivious to the green spots on his own face. Not to pat my own back, but it was excellent work. Like someone had taken a highlighter and gone to town.

Someone laughed. I pretended to read my book when another person noticed. It wasn't long before people were covering their mouths and snickering, and I was trying so hard not to lose control or give myself away. But it was a bit too excellent.

By the time Chaz took a seat with his cronies, the dots on his face had grown, multiplied, and ripened to a bright, radioactive sheen. I could only stare, in awe of what I'd done. Me and everyone else.

Chairs scraped the floor. Soon Chaz found himself alone at the table, looking at his arms as a buzz came over the cafeteria.

Chaz's sunken eyes emerged from their pits as nuclear splotches formed on his skin. First dots, then spots, until he was covered completely. He pulsed to life, neon and glowing. By then it was bedlam, kids stood on chairs to get a better view. People snapped pictures and videos. Only, the laughter quickly turned to fear. Someone pulled the fire alarm. Greenie, the hall monitor, came rushing to see what was going on, skidding to a halt when he saw poor old radioactive Chaz.

Perhaps I'd overdone it. I kept my head down when the EMTs arrived, my face buried in a book as Chaz was laid out on a gurney, crying like a baby, his spiky hair matted down on one side as he called for his mommy. By then, no one was laughing. I slunk low in my chair.

When Mr. Wolff arrived, the school was cleared out. The rumors started about a biological attack. Covid-22. A new pandemic was underway.

Oops.

Now, out in the yard, it's a bit concerning how quickly my brother has put things together. Still, there isn't much he can do about it. Is there?

My smile fades. It seems like Colton is contemplating the unthinkable. Someone bumps into me from behind, but I manage to keep my eyes locked on my brother. "Wait. You're not...you're not going to tell Mom and Dad, are you?"

He rolls his neck like he does when he's nervous. As the minivan mishap clears out and the procession gets going again, Greenie barks at the stragglers to form a line. My stomach rolls at the thought of my brother actually considering ratting me out.

But how could Colton rat me out? He, of all people, should know what it would sound like, running to the parentals and telling them his little sister is casting spells on bullies. Still, this change in the tide makes me squirm.

"Oh man, this is what I was worried about." He nods toward the parking lot, and I follow his gaze, where I find the reason for his nerves. Jada Johnson, my old journalism mentor, now a freshman reporter, is storming across the lot, headed our way.

Yikes. In the distance, the doors to Peakland High School swing open and kids come waltzing out, joking and blinking at the bright sunshine. Oh boy. It appears the entire Peakland school system is getting an early dismissal thanks to yours truly.

"Colton. Abby."

Jada waves us down, her phone in her hand, poised and ready to capture incriminating evidence. Colton scans the lot as though looking for an escape route. "Great, just what we need." He looks at me. "This needs to go away. Tonight."

I nod. Sure, I hold all the smarts in the family, but some situations call for brawn. Or in Colton's case, scrawn.

"It will," I assure him.

Jada's closing in. She's about to start with the rapid fire questions. *Hit 'em fast and hit 'em hard. And* never *let up,* she used to say last year when she was an eighth grader and took me under her wing.

Thankfully Dad pulls up in the van. "Hey kids, um, everything all right?"

I smile at his timing. Jada stops in her tracks, leveling a gaze at us. She cocks her head as though to say *This isn't over*.

That was close.

Acknowledgments

I set out to write a football book, and I did, I think. But something else happened along the way. While this is no memoir, a certain trait found its way into the story. One I recognized all too well.

My dad is to blame for my genetics, but also to thank for those Sunday afternoons we spent watching football games together. Over spilled sodas and overturned bowls of chips, I learned the ins and outs of the game, soaked up the over the top antics and silliness that were the eighties, and, at least when my stepmother was in the room, got acquainted with some choice words and colorful language.

Thanks to Diane Fanning, for cleaning up all my messes—both in the kitchen and on the page. To Liz Nichols, the real life Abby. To Dad, for being my hero. To Sarah Miller, whose feedback on early drafts made this such a better book. To the entire Immortal Works team, especially Staci Olsen, for believing in my work, and Holli Anderson, who whipped this story into something worth reading.

Thanks to all the support from friends and family. For years I wrote by myself. Now it feels like I write with all of you.

Lastly, thanks to Bella, Simon, and Anne, my three favorite nonfictional characters.

About the Author

Pete Fanning is the author of *Justice in a Bottle* and *Runaway Blues*. He lives in Virginia with his wife, son, baby girl, and two very spoiled dogs. He can be found at www.petefanning.com, where he's posted over 200 flash fiction stories.

This has been an
Immortal Production

www.ingramcontent.com/pod-product-compliance
Lightning Source LLC
Chambersburg PA
CBHW032016050726
47590CB00006B/2197